Billion's

Percy Stevenson

Published by Percy Stevenson, 2024.

BILLION'S

First edition. November 1, 2024.

Copyright © 2024 Percy Stevenson.

ISBN: 979-8227572646

Written by Percy Stevenson.

For the little people who are trod on every day of their lives.

Billion's ... By Percy Stevenson

...

For those who work withing the finance sector in London's stock exchange, envy and greed are brought into the open when large amounts of money are transferred to within their sphere of influence, and with normally managing vast sums to be able invest in large projects, but then told that this American lump is ring fenced for other purposes, this rings bells in the heads of financiers and bankers, they all know that this is a ghost dump sent to them to be cleaned and then sent back to where it came from in the New York City Wall Street stock exchange

In the minds of mice and men a plan is brewing to take a little and run, but how to get away with such a scam, some regard themselves as being smart, and so a plan is put forward to the committee and voted on, the conclusion being that they can blame someone else and escape in the dust this snatch will inevitably cause in the city of London, so it's a go for plan A to start.

All hold on for the ride of their lives, because this has not been done before and failure is unthinkable, with the right timing it could take weeks before they realize their loss.

Innocent minds don't realize the mess they are in, it takes a practical mechanic to give them the reality of this bad news, money is power and with so much lost it becomes a death sentence.

CHAPTER 1 ... FRANK WARRAN CARS ... EAST LONDON.

Billy is fitting a new gearbox into a Jaguar on the high ramp, JoJo, the apprentice is trying to help but losing concentration as Billy tries to locate the splines on the first motion shaft in the clutch housing, both grunting with the effort.

"Down your end Joe."

"I am down."

"Ok, we pull it out and check on the clutch alignment, where's the tool?"

"At the side of you Bill, near the front wheel."

Billy grunted as he pulled out the gearbox and with Joes hand placed it on the high stand.

"Ok, Joe, take five, let's check this out."

They stood looking at each other and gasping with the effort of holding the heavy gearbox above their heads for so long.

JoJo passed him the spline aligning tool and watched as Billy checked the alignment and the angle.

"Is it the right gearbox?"

"Yes Bill, according to the part numbers, it's bang on."

"And I suppose its second hand, right?"

Joe grinned and nodded to the office door, "Bald eagle won't pay for a new one, you know it makes sense mate."

Billy had to agree with him and double checked the alignment again, "So why the hell won't it go in?"

"Maybe the bearing in the fly wheel is knackered?"

Billy put his finger in the flywheel center, "Yep, there's the problem, ok, down with the box and we'll have to find a new bearing."

Both grunted again as they lowered the gearbox to the floor.

"Ok, go find the bearing box in the office and tell Frank we need extra time on this one, I'll find the puller to get it out."

JoJo disappeared into the office just as the roller shutter doors rattled.

"Hollo, who is it?"

"Me Billy, Sandra, we've had a bank statement and it's all your fault!"

He pressed the button to raze up the door and as soon as she had space to enter, she was on him and shouting.

"You, stupid little git, the bank's got the hump with us and now our mortgaged application is down the tubes Billy, so what the hell have you done?"

She picked up the broom and chased him into the garage.

He held her off as she shouted at him.

"Nothing, I bought a new battery for the van, that's it, nothing else babe!"

She waved the paper at him as she fumed, but to get a better grip of the broom hand to hit him she handed the paper to JoJo, who had just come back through the office door.

He read it and scratched his head in confusion then returned to the office allowing the door to close behind him and for Billy to sort out his own domestic issue.

She was trying to batter him with the broom when an announcement came over the Tannoy system.

"Will William Bonkers please come the office!"

She stopped her aggression and shouted at him again, "Tell him Billy, he's taking the piss in there, so do something and now!"

"Calm Babe, it's not me, so let's go and sort it out in a civilized way, yes?"

She slammed the brush down and marched off to the office, Billy following her.

She entered the smelly space of Franks office and stared at him, "What a pig hole this place is, and what's that smell in here?"

"Just work Sandra, come and sir down please, so have you read this statement from the bank?"

"Yeah, they're pissed at us for something."

"Sandra, it's a statement of how much you currently have in your account, did you read that it?"

"Well, I looked at the noughts and thought that Billy had bought something again, that's why I'm here, I was going to batter him!"

"Sandra, you and Billy have one hundred and twenty million in your account, did you not see that?"

Her mouth drooped as she listened to him, "But that's impossible!"

Billy took the paper from Frank and looked at his bank account numbers, he turned to Frank and shook his head in disbelief.

The man at the counter coughed and nodded to the paper from the bank, "Err ... I couldn't help noticing the noughts on the end of your statement and you have nine noughts."

Billy turned to him, "And that means?"

"Well, you don't have 120 million in your bank, you have 120 billion in your current account dear, understood?"

"Really?" Billy had to sit down; his head was spinning.

"Impossible!" said Sandra.

"How?" squeaked Billy.

"It's a scam Billy," said Frank, "Someone is pulling a fast one, that can't be real money, can it?"

"It's a snatch!" said the customer.

"So, Mr Wilson, you know about these things, so what the hell is going on here?"

Mr Wilson smiled and continued, "Well, I my opinion Frank, what you have here is a ghost dump being snatched, someone's prime is being washed in the London stock exchange and has been, for want of another word diverted to the lads account, to pick up later I would say."

Frank scrutinized the speaker to get a handle on the snatch, "But they have just given the lad 120 billion pounds, just like that, how the hell can they do that?"

"Please don't think for a moment that this is a mistake, they don't make mistakes like this in the city, no, this is a calculated snatch of a big lump of finance from the city's big league players, so the lad is in deep trouble, people get killed for this kind of finance, I would suggest he starts negotiations to return it as soon as possible, and perhaps that would keep him alive, or even start to employ a protection contractor for his personal security."

"Security!" screeched Sandra, "Do you mean that they would kill Billy for this?"

"Madam," said Mr Wilson, "Someone is expecting to still be earning from this finance in its warm 5% accounts, and if I were them, I'd be mighty put out, understand?"

He took out his phone and started his calculations, "By my rough calculations, during this conversation you have just earned very nearly a 100 grand in interest, understood?"

"But that's bonkers!"

Sandra sat down with Billy as they both thought about the problem, Billy was studying the people in the waiting room as he worked it out in his brain.

Frank butted into the conversation, "So, Mr Wilson, what is it you do for a living sir?"

"Well, my prime responsibility is for investment banking in the city, new builds, upturned restructuring of businesses under threat from takeovers, and generally, things like that."

"Look Frank, the boy is in real trouble here, this will be missed and very quickly by its real owners, get it? These players are the top of the tree, understood, I suggest you contact the bank and claim ignorance or something!"

Another customer stands and walks into the conversation, "No, don't do that, it would be a fatal mistake, you see this must be in the wash tub for the offshore investor, he'll be mad initially but then he'll panic, because if this is discovered to be a working system in the within the city, the whole edifice could crumble, for this kind of thing to become public, governments fail, questions asked in the house of commons, agencies sent to keep the lid on it all, understood here Frank? Mr Wilson is correct, the kid needs serious protection, or the dominoes start to fall as this becomes bad news in the city, in fact, for us to be here with the kid, could mean our deaths as well, they have to keep the lid on this at all costs, understood?"

Mr Wilson smiled at the man as Billy watched their faces, "They need Mr Bloodworth, don't they Gerald, his is the collection agency isn't it?"

The man smiled back at Mr Wilson, "Absolutely Mr Wilson and bloody hope he hasn't already been contacted and given the task of recovery!"

"What the hell is happening here Billy?" screeched Sandra again.

"But this is just dosh pinged into my account, I ping it back, so what?"

A third customer stood up and walked over and into their conversation, "Wrong, this is power lost by morons, so we are all piggies in the middle and will be destroyed simply because we are witnesses to the loss of the ghost dump, clear everyone?"

Frank stared at the third man for a second or two before speaking "And you are sir?"

The man took out a wallet and showed him a little card identification with security photo imbedded into it

Frank read it out loud, "Mr Wayland Smith, Homeland Department MOD section Whitehall, he handed it back to the man.

"Look, this has to be done and quick, lockdown the building, every door every phone call, the sooner Mr Bloodworth gets here with his support and security, the better, right gentlemen?" he turned to the other two customers.

"But I have the cash and carry to do?" said Sandra.

Mr Smith turned to again, "Look, we are all dead for being here with you, all of us will have to be cleared for them to feel safe and that's if the dump is discovered, we have to survive at all costs!"

"But I have things to do, the shop, the stall, I have family to sort!" said Sandra.

Billy shut her up with a growl, "Sandra, for once in your life, shut the fuck up, I feel we have to trust these people for now, so give it a rest woman and listen up, ok, Mr Smith, if you know this man then make the call, yes?"

Billy locked eyes with his boss Frank as he watched these people and listened as Mr Smith made the call, his brain clicked round one click at a time, Smith was now waiting for an answer down the line, "Mr Bloodworth's office please, yes, me, I'm Wayland Smith, level two Whitehall security sector, I require a full tactical protection unit please from unknow x-rays, yes dear fully understood, I'll wait on the end of this line then, thank you so much dear."

He turned to see the faces of fear watching his every move.

So, you two gentlemen work in the city, any ideas who would be capable of doing such a thing?"

"This is just bollocks Billy, let's just be gone from here, this whole thing is scarring me!" screeched Sandra.

Billy locked eyes again with his boss, "Frank, you could check them out couldn't you, a call down east would do it, right?"

"And involved some very nasty people lad, not a smart move, imagine if Jimmy the saw got hold of this little lot, we'd be fish food withing the hour, and so would these gentlemen, he has the muscle to defend such a sum from anyone who wants trouble, we are just the minions here lad!"

Mr Smith smiled at the idea, "Now that's a great idea, you could call for help, perhaps give them a sniff and we could all disappear in the smoke of corruption from on high."

"I want out of here Billy, to hell with all of them!" said Sandra again.

Billy continued to star at the man.

But Smith continued with his speech, "Now look here people, if you go home now after receiving that letter from the bank then they know the cats out of the bag and in the open, alarm bells will be ringing all over the city and we will be picked up in the street, and you will be worked on for information, possibly thinking that this is an outside country trying to kill city links, the people in the media will jump on the story and all of us will be obvious villains, we'll be smeared with allegations of being connected to the bad side of London, through Franks connections, even your families won't want to help after they've destroyed our lives, clear here people?"

"So, who could these people be her Mr Smith, foreigners?" asked Frank.

"Look, we have three ways out of this, so let's think this through a moment, firstly we have the people who've lost the dump, and after all we have to assume it's a secret dump, from offshore somewhere, but the internal enquiry will start, managers, sales and investments."

"Secondly, they'll want this hushed up, because if this breaks, it'll break the banking system her in the UK because this is money laundering, on a very big scale, right?"

"From where?" asked Frank.

Mr Smith shrugged, "My guess it's American money slipped into the system by friendly stockbrokers on the floor in Wall Street and the city of London."

"American gangsters then?" asked Sandra.

"International drug money then?" said Frank.

Mr Smith shrugged again, "Perhaps, but the real problem is that they are exposed, and they will kill us all because of that, recovered or not, we are all doomed."

"Unless I talk the boy's uptown?" said Frank.

"It would help us to become invisible, we could escape as they investigated your friends, right?"

"You, are bonkers, if the lads up the west end hear about this, we had better be a very long way from here, understood?"

"We could give them a sniff and be gone, do you see that, Frank?"

"You don't even know these people, you're a shiny arse from the London set, you do not understand real violence do you boy?"

"We could negotiate and come out quite rich if we work it right, give the lump back perhaps and just take a slice of commission?"

Billy had finally worked them out and his jawline said it all, "Never! We will all have to be killed for them to feel safe!"

"Billy!" screeched Sandra.

"We have to live and survive Sand, let me just come up with a plan here."

"But Billy, these people are experts!"

"But how much are you keeping son?"

"All of it Frank, are you with me on this?"

Frank grinned back at him, "Bonkers by name and nature aren't you Billy boy, they'll fight you for this, you do know that?"

"And you are with me then?"

"I have no choice it seems, still, very interesting eh boy?"

"But Billy!" screeched Sandra again.

"All of it Sand, the whole bloody lot, we are the ones who pay them now, clear?"

"Billy!"

"They won't get a squeaky fart from me Sand, all of it, understood, he's right over there, the bigger the money the bigger the power, now that's me, understood?

She stood up with hands on her hips and stared at him, but he had suddenly changed, the mantle of leadership and determination was in his eyes, and she spotted it first.

"The only way Billy boy, they have to earn every payout, to keep control of them all yes?"

"We, glorious few!" said Gerald, "We stand as family or die in the gutter with discontent and failure, to be trodden under the feet of men."

All faces turned to Gerald and listened to his poetic words.

"Moron!" said Sandra.

Suddenly Mr Smith's phone buzzed into life and the room fell silent.

Smith answered the phone, "Yes, yes that's me sir, Wayland Smith level two, contacts and commissions from Whitehall 101 sir! Well, many years ago sir, we worked together, I need a code for red cover from you in protection from unknown bandits, this in fact could well be your retirement contract, the big one at last sir.

"Well, I'm at Frank Warren cars, please knock on the roller shutter doors four times sir, I have directed these people to a complete lockdown until your arrival, just you by the way, because this is very sensitive ...... err Smith level two Whitehall Mr Bloodworth, I helped you out with information one time when you and your people had problems, please do not inform your employers until we have had a conversation face to face, I'll explain it all sir when you arrive, yes sir, Wayland Smith sir!" He closed the call and looked around at the faces staring at him, "What?"

And what's stopping him from killing us all and taking the dosh?" asked Billy.

Smith turned to Gerald, "So, what's stopping him taking the money?"

Gerald turned to Billy, "Well because Billy is now the key to all this and he must quickly consider his options, he might have already received calls for this recovery, but I imagine that he's a clever man, and he would have worked out that this could be a can of worms, he'll be curious however, and that's our timing to get him involved, slowly, slowly, catches the monkey, right?"

"And this Blood bloke can sort this?"

"We do not want this man to trade us in to his bosses, he has a department for the problems in our society, he organises and plans operation to rid out Nation of problem people, he normally works for the government in such matters, so we must entrap him in this to gain his trust and obligations for our protection, understand everyone?"

"So, you're say, that he kills people for the government?" asked Billy.

Smith turned to the faces watching him, "Education and realities of our systems can be shocking, he's the ultimate third party contracts company who rid us of problems, and is so secret in government circles that not even the Prime Minister is aware of this department, he contracts people from prison to do the work, what, you never thought that our government would do such a thing? Grow up, you lot, this is management responsibilities of running a country of seventy million people, get it?"

Billy gulped in understanding the people in the room.

Frank asked, "And we can trust a known killer, just like that?"

"Yes, we must, he is a man of his word, we employ him for our safety, so this must work, he is known to be very strict with his employees, all known killers, you see."

"And a wink and a handshake can do this?" asked Frank.

"Yes, if he's in he's in and we will be safe, he is well respected within the industry and no one does him wrong, it's very dangerous to cross this man, understand everyone?"

"And, if he say's sod off, then what do we do?"

"Well, he'll fall in line with the authorities and get the money back anyway he can, then all hell breaks loose as the secret bubbles up in the city, I'll let out a whisper and of course he himself could then be put on a new snuff list, after all, he's now involved, right?"

"Shit, I don't like this, Billy!" screeched Sandra.

"So, you lot drag this man into our swamp, just like that, I'd be bloody fuming mate," said Billy.

The roller shutter door suddenly banged a couple of times and brought them all out of their discussion, but Frank reacted to the noise, "Piss off Abdul, your clutches are too expensive, and the last one was crap!"

The parts delivery man shouted through to him, "But this one's VOR Frank, I can't send it back, it's yours, special order, remember?"

"Tomorrow Abdul, anyway the Audi isn't here yet, deliver it tomorrow!"

"But they'll scratch you off the delivery route, I'll tell em you weren't in, yes?"

"Yes mate, tomorrow! Food poisoning or something!"

"I'll put you on last recall for tomorrow, Frank, but you owe me a drink for this!"

"Yes Abdul, drinks on me, anyway, aren't you Muslim, aren't you supposed to not drink?"

"Only on fast days Frank."

You're making it up as you go along Abdul!"

The door was now silent, but Billy broke the spell, "Families, what about families?"

Frank stared around the room at the faces watching Billy.

"Billy, we wait for an expert's opinion, best way I think, and not to make stupid moves at this time, yes?"

"Yes Frank, we have to think about this one," he locked eyes with Frank again, "But what a coincidence we have here, bankers, security man, all too comfortable isn't it?"

"And you are saying Billy?"

"These wankers are all connected, this is a setup, run and planned by them, it's funny how they know about your links up west? So, what do we have here Mr Smith, the first part of your plan to call in the muscle to grind us down, correct?"

"It's a straightforward heist then Billy?"

"Absolutely boss, these people think they can run rings round us."

"Running rings around us, eh?"

"Innocents, eh boss? So, what comes next, the guns or the beatings?" So where are we in the plan so far Mr Smith, A or B?"

Smith smiled at him and breathed out before answering him, "Quick, very quick, we thought that we could negotiate and perhaps make you and your wife very rich."

"And look guilty as well, eh?"

"No not at all Billy."

"So, we the villains with obvious links to criminals have had this plan for years officer, oh, well done, you can tell that they are real criminals here officer."

"We would have informed you of the realities in the end Billy."

"Yeah, as the old bill slammed on the cuffs, obvious a criminal enterprise officer, we were just blackmailed into helping them, glad to help sir, our civic duty officer!"

"But you are in a very strong position you know? We just want a little to take up investment offers in the city, all very above board."

"Yes, all very neat but the dosh is in my bank, nice and safe."

"We were not expecting an argument here Billy, after all we are the advisers for what to do with all this wealth."

"My wealth and my blame, eh? All his planning officer, nasty piece of work if you ask me officer, you can see it on his face he's a thieving little bastard! So, I take the heat and you lot slide off to the sun, Spain, France, possibly even south America, eh?"

"So, lads, how many in the crew?" asked Frank as he stared at them.

"Also, very quick Frank, and also unexpected, you people are very sharp."

"He's as thick as a brick!" shouted Sandra.

Frank ignored her shout and glared at him as he waited for his answer.

"Ok, there are five of us, my job was to eliminate or get a guard dog to give us time to escape their wrath, failing that we just make a break for it, anywhere just gone."

"Bankers, wankers more like, big eyes, and big heads, and stupid fat bellies thinking you could take all this and run?"

"That's not the point Sand, we are the targets, Frank, me and you, we're here to take the blame and the jail time! You can smell crime on them officer!" said Billy.

"Certainly not, the plan was for everyone to escape with a clean billion each, then split to wherever we wanted, a clean and equitable split, that's it, but we didn't think it would be."

"So much eh, a big old lump to hide eh lads?" said Frank.

Billy looked to him again, "So should we involve Jimmy the saw?"

Frank ignored his question as he focused on the three of them, "So you lot can play this financial game then?"

"All for one and one for all!" said Gerald.

"So, the five musketeers, really, oh do me a favour!" said Billy.

Gerald smiled again at Billy, "Look we wanted Mr Bloodworth to be like a referee, he could oversee the equitable release of the funds, as well as being the enforcer to keep us from being too greedy."

"Morons!" squeaked Sandra.

"And Mr Smith's opinion of these office boys?" asked Frank.

Smith shrugged, "Look I have to level with you, this whole thing was forced on me by my brothers, my younger brother Max is the one who transferred the money over to you, I had to come up with a plan and quick, your name fitted into his computer program, together with your boss here and his obvious links up west."

"Greed then?" said Frank.

"His idea, the problem however is obvious, he transferred too much in one go, a couple of bills, would have been enough, so the fault is his, I'm afraid."

"And your other brother?" asked Frank.

Smith thumbed to Gerald who grinned back at him.

"So, answer me this please gentlemen, is Mr Bloodworth connected in any way to you boys?"

"No!" said Gerald, "That was his idea," he nodded to Wayland Smith."

"And that's your real name?"

"Yes, Wayland, we have an American mother."

"Bonkers, the lot of them!" said Sandra.

"I knew him from when I worked over there," said Smith.

"So, this whole plan is based on the fact that you can trust this man Bloodworth, who you tell us is a killer, now that was a hell of a risk lads, really?"

"We know how they will react in the banking sector; they'll be quiet, and the internal enquiry will be silent as it works through the system, too big a dump to lose track of you see?"

"And you idiots wouldn't think they would be able to track you and the money down?"

"Our brother Max is very smart on the split; he has big plans for it."

"You're idiots, didn't you realise how nasty these people can be?"

"But we can buy them, we have the wealth, and as you know, everyone is bribe able, it's just a question of how much, right?"

"Using this bloke Bloodworth?"

"Yes!"

"Frank!" said Sandra, "These people have shit for brains, what do we do now?"

"No Sand, he's right," said Billy, "Money no object anymore, we can bribe anyone we like, there's plenty to go round after all, correct?"

"And traceable Billy, any account can be traced, and don't think we can put it in an offshore account just like that, we need time to do things like that."

"So, you know the banking rules madam?" asked Gerald.

"Surprised? I've been doing money all my life, this will be just another lump to move here and there."

"Never had it before have you babe, this is going to be interesting gents!" said Billy.

"No, not this much, but it's just numbers, I can do that."

Billy smiled at her, "My darling girls is capable with money, me, well I just spend it, but Sandra here is in another league, now that must be surprising right?"

The bankers stared at them in silence, Gerald coughed before speaking, "Err .... We are very useful in such circumstances you know; we have links that can help!"

"I don't trust the fuckers, Billy!"

"My darling girl hits the nail on the head yet again, trust, so how do we work this?"

CHAPTER 2 ... CITY OF LONDON ... STOCK EXCHANGE ... BANKING FLOOR.

Mr Desmond Simperate watched them all as a slave master should, he didn't use first names, and sometimes he just used grunts and so the moral on the floor was as low as it could be among the traders, he ruled with a rod of iron and expected results from their trading.

"New York is down Ned, so that'll be our fault, right?"

"Well, you normally Maxwell, what did he call you last time, an incompetent degenerate with turpitude induced brain patterns."

Max laughed at him, "I almost believe him, he's probably right, so, anyway, I need time to do the deed, are you ready?"

"Ready for what?"

"Look, I need five in his corner office, I have his codes, but I need his laptop to confirm, understand?"

"So, my job is what?"

"Well, go and make a scene, a big one, nice and loud, the whole nine yards, clear?"

"Doing what?"

"Oh, just kick over his precious coffee machine, kick the bastard thing to bits if needed."

"But he'll sack me!"

Max grinned, "Yes, but it's a price I am willing to pay, and besides, if you look at the clock, we only have half an hour before New York shuts down, and that might give us 24 hours to split, get me, Mr Nedlington?"

"You are such a bastard Mr Smith!"

"I'm simply returning a favor Ned; he might be nicer to people in the future."

Ned looked at their floor manager and locked eyes with him, "Err ... I think not Beagley puppy."

Max elbowed him to get it done then went back to his computer face panel.

"Coffee anyone, I'm todays big spender, despite losing the Glenfield account."

The girls on the screens laughed and placed their hands in the air for his generosity.

He winked at Max and walked off to the machine, then flicked coins into the slot.

He turned to Max and then kicked the machine, "Robing bastard, the thing has ripped me off yet again!" he kicked it again then took hold of it and shook the thing, "Why can't we have a machine that works?"

"Hey, stop that Nedlington, that machine is my property and is only a curtesy for workers on this floor."

"Yes sir, but it's just took my money, yet again and I'm not having it anymore!" he gave it another kick.

Mr Simperate walked over and tried to stop him from shaking the machine, but Ned was in a rage as the machine fell over, and coffee powder and hot water splashed everywhere but mostly over his boss, Mr Simperate.

Ned kicked it again as out of the corner of his eye he saw Max disappear into the corner office.

"If you continue with this aggression, you will be fired Mr Nedlington!"

"Sorry Desperate, but it was the last straw, that was my last change, so now I have to scrounge more from the girls, and you know how tight they are?"

"How dare you use that name in relation to me Nedlington, I will not be made fun of on my own floor!"

Mr Simperate was now jumping up and down with the sudden splash of hot water and coffee over his clean white shirt.

"Now that must be hot Desperate!"

The girls were now full of laughter at the scene and Mr Simperate was screeching in pain and anger.

"That's it, you are fired, get out of this building, your P45 will be posted to you along with any money due to your incompetent trading."

"You probably need some butter on that Desperate, you could try some of Betty's butter, because Betty's butter is a bit bitter, so Betty's bitter butter could be better, well, in the long run anyway."

"Out!" screeched Mr Simperate, "Get out and be gone from my floor!"

Max was in a rush to find the account of his boss's laptop, time was not on his side as he listened to the row now breaking out near the coffee machine, then he found it and quickly punched in the code to transfer the finance to his coded number in London.

Ned was slowing down with his argument and Max knew he had very little time to complete the transfer as he listened, so he pressed and kept his finger on the numbers transfer, but the computer pinged the end of its download.

Ned was still causing mayhem on the floor as he gave their boss some more advice with being scalded by hot water, "Perhaps a shower would be advisable sir, and not the monthly one you normally enjoy?"

"How dare you Nedlington, I'm calling security, you are fired young man, so be gone!"

Max was now at their side and trying to comfort his boss, "Just an accident Desperate, he's just not the technical type, he, doesn't understand the instructions!"

"And you are also fired Mr Smith, your incompetence is ruining my averages, you can also be gone from this building, good riddance and now!"

"But sir, the clock, New York will be waiting sir!"

"Get out, the pair of you, I'll make the call to New York, you and him, are both fired, now get out!"

The giggling of the girls stopped as Mr Simperate glared at them into silence, he then waved for Max and Ned to be gone from his trading floor.

In the lift Max laughed at Ned's advice given to their boss, "Butter?"

"Oh, my old grans advice, butter's the thing, cuts, burns, just dab with butter."

"But what that about Betty?"

"A tongue twister, a bit of Betty's bitter butter must be better, right?"

Max had to laugh at him as the lift descended.

"So?" asked Ned, "The final score is what?"

"Well, he had 12 on the key, so I just pressed the zeros until the thing pinged stop."

"So how much in the end then?"

Max shrugged, "12 mill I think, but it might be more."

"Off the scale then so what's the max out number?"

Max shrugged again, "Don't know Mr Nedlington, perhaps more than we thought, we'll just have to ask our new best buddy!"

"Is he?"

"I don't know, never met the bloke, a mechanic we think, he's just the right name you see, and with helpful friend down the west end."

"A gangster?"

"Perhaps, anyway, Gerry thinks he can point and take the credit as well if the law intervenes."

"Personally, I think that this bloke will have a brain in his head, so we just need to negotiate as transfer fee, then move on."

"That's a risk though Max?"

"What with city low life's, what risk would it be?"

"So, you lot are hoping for a nice boy to pay off, right?"

"A good mechanic I'm told!"

"And you've just given him 12 million, just like that?"

"Well, I must have put him in a good mood, right, we just have to ask him to sign our check, bing, bang, bosh!"

"So how much each then?"

"Two mill each, then we split, and get lost."

"But old desperate will feel their wrath, right?"

"Oh, yes, they'll towel slap his arse for a while, and then find us, so we had better find a bit of Betty's better butter and be gone by then, yes?"

"But he has friends on high, his uncle will protect him, right?"

"Not from something like this Ned, the mans doomed," Max waved a door key in his face and laughed.

"And?"

"Well old Desperate is having a very bad day, he's even being burgled as we speak, fancy leaving your door key in your coat pocket, lazy, right?"

"Oh yes Maximillion, very lazy!"

"My new nick name?"

"Well, you earned it boy, so how long before the truth hit's home?"

"We have twenty-four hours and then the news will come in from New York like a whirlwind, transfer officers will alarm the exchange, and all hell will break loose, but we've been fired right, so it can't be us, can it?"

"But if it's picked up by New York before closure, then what?"

"We have to move faster and involve obvious suspects."

"I don't get you Max?"

Max laughed again as the lift stopped on the ground floor, he waved the key again, "You see, he's not being burgled he's going to receive presents, bada bing, bada bong!"

"You, are going to plant evidence?"

"Yep, poor old desperate, how bad can it get?" he burst out laughing again as Ned followed him out of the building and onto the London street.

CHAPTER 3 ... WALL STREET FOREIGN EXCHANGE ... NEW YORK CITY.

In the corner office of the New York trading floor, Robert Vigo made an emergency call to the finance director of a firm that only had one client. "Hello, oh, hello sir, this is Bobby down on Wall street exchange floor, yes sir, I am legally obliged to inform you of a slight loss on the London exchange, well London has mislaid a large sum, possible a computer black out sir."

He listened to instructions before carrying on with the conversation.

"Oh, it's from out stock fund sir, yes sir 120 billion sir!"

He held the phone at arm's length as the swearing continued down the line, "Oh, we do have a transfer link sir, we can chase it down, no problems sir!"

He held the phone away from his ear again as the man fumed down the line.

"Just some lazy ass secretary sir, elbows on the laptop obviously, or just some confusion."

"Yes sir, on it now, oh, how much sir? Well, we calculate that were down half a mill per day in interest, but we can claw it back sir, I'll blain London for this clusterfuck sir, they'll pay up no problem!"

"I just need to get over there and kick some ass sir!"

He placed the phone down and breathed out slowly having informed the client, then pressed his intercom, "Listen up Julie, get me on a plane to London as quick as you can, then call Winstanley for me and arrange for him to pick me up at Heathrow, tell his I need his help to find a loss, he's on commission as well, add that please, we need this guy sweet, ok?"

He sat back in his chair and breathed out slowly again as he wondered how he was going to handle this in London, he looked at the photos of his family on his desk top and breathed out some more, he fully realized that if he didn't come back with the goods, he might not survive the week, and he sat and bitterly regrated working for these people, he knew that he had to come up with a plan to escape their anger at him, because he fully understood, it would be all his fault, no matter how he conducted the chase.

He was pulled out of his depression by the phone ringing at his side, "Err yes Julie?"

"A Mr John Winstanley on the line sir, do you want to take it, or are you on route?"

"I'll take it Julie .... yes John, you have questions obviously?"

"Hi Bobby, so what's the big deal over here?"

"Well, we have a great deal of money lost to the London stock exchange and think it's a snatch, the problem however is this, my clients wanted anonymity from disclosure to where the money came from, get my meaning?"

"Ah, mob money?"

"Correct, so we have to be very delicate in finding the thieves and returning the finance to its rightful owners, or heads might roll, get it?"

"Oh, yes Bobby, I got ya, so when do I expect you to arrive?"

"As soon as I can catch a flight, in the meantime could you search some of your contacts for clues, and perhaps interview the floor manager, his name is ...."

Bobby read the name in his book before answering, "A Mr A Simperate, thirteenth floor, we want to know how, when and most importantly, the who, clear?"

"Unlucky for some eh, so how much?"

"John, I cannot disclose the amount over an open line, sorry, but I can tell you that your commission will be your retirement fund, no probs!"

"Really?"

"Hunt them down please John, we need this, and God damned fast, get it?"

CHAPTER 4 ... WARREN CARS ...
RECEPTION AREA.

Billy leaned on the counter and whispered into Franks ear, "So how is this going to go boss?"

"You have to play this by ear boy, and don't make any mistakes, this could be the end of us if you handle this thing wrong, understand?"

"Yes Frank, so what about this Blood bloke?"

"A great respect is needed here son, careful let's hear what he has to say first, but as you can see, these idiot are counting on him and his system, so don't let him walk away with empty pockets, yes?"

"Yes boss, very clear."

"We're in, like it or not, so plan for our survival at any cost."

"Down to me then?"

"Yes, Billy boy, it's all down to you, are you ready?"

Billy nodded to him, and Frank nodded back

Frank took his time in assessing his clients now sitting as if they had no worries in the world.

Smith shouted over to them at the counter, "So you have an opinion then, could you share it with us perhaps?"

Billy stared in his direction, "So, the pre plan is what, we're all snuffed in the end?"

"Not in any plan son!" said Smith, "Look here, you are a very rich man, you could buy an army if you so desired, you have money and as said before, money is power!"

"So, you can just point and pretend to care in front of your banker friends, right?"

"I think that you are wasted as a grease monkey son, you have the foresight of a planner and it's a natural talent we have just witnessed here, don't worry, you'll come out of this with a great deal of wealth."

"If I survive though eh?"

Frank coughed at the back of him, "Do you know Billy, I don't think these boys are what they seem, lies upon lies, so what do you think their real plan is?"

"For them to be rich I have to die, now that must be part of their plan, but then we have our secret weapon, my girl Sandra, now that, is not in their plan, no sir, real trouble with her I think."

"Not so young man, not in anyone's plan!" said Gerald.

"You have to give them credit though boss, they had you checked out, now that must have been hard, so who do we know that would give you away like that?" said Billy.

Smith grinned at them, "The Mayfair club, in the West End, the barman, and he has a great memory of people coming and going."

Frank smiled back at him before he spoke, "Billy, they don't know us yet do they, they're ahead at the moment but all things change eh?"

"Oh yes boss, all things change! So, they really wanted you to go down the West End route Frank, more smoke and mirrors."

"I am so impressed with you son, smarter than the average mechanic!"

Sandra growled before speaking, "I'm so sick of this," she pointed to Gerald "You, cut the crap and tell us the plan and how you're going to chug it all down and into what account?"

Billy thumbed to her, "Ups, lads, here we go, best come over with some good news."

Gerald smiled at her, "London's finest, eh? You really are the surprise of the day madam."

Sandra fiddled with her little handbag and pulled out an old, dog-eared card from the bottom.

"Ok, smart arse, let's have a demo of your action, by transferring 10 bill into that account!"

Gerald smiled again at her, he looked at the card in surprise, and you have a Swiss account, really?"

"Sandra?" asked Billy, "You have a Swiss bank account?"

"Shut up, where the hell do you think we come from Billy, my granddad was involved in the Brinks Mat snatch, only he wasn't caught, like the morons who went on spending sprees, and were swept up like little lambs, grandad gave this to us at the wedding, this was for an extreme emergency, so I think that this is it, yes?"

"Oh yes babe, this is definitely it."

"Shut up knob head, if we don't scrape something from this, they'll leave us for dead with diddly squat as they sun themselves on a nice warm Spanish beach,"

"And besides Sandra, this is their test of loyalty to the plan, correct?" said Frank, from behind his countertop.

"Yes Frank, let's call it the test of their loyalty to us and the big money."

"Exactly Sandra, after all we still have a hundred and ten bill still in the pocket, right?"

"Yes Frank, so you lot, this is a sign of trust in us, so put that into your calculations and get the transaction done, and I warn you here, if you upset my boy over there, you will not get one squeaky fart from him, he's gets very mardy if you upset him, understood?"

"Calm darling, it's not a problem, we can do this, and trust it is, and a very good idea as well, so let me start the transfer, good for you, so the name of the bank dear?"

She snorted at him for calling her darling, "Ok, The Grand Foreign exchange of Zurich, in William Strasser."

"Really, ok madam, let me start."

"And she won't be fooled by your numbers trickery, so if my girl is upset then so am I, can I be more clear gents?" said Billy.

Gerald started laughing at her conversation but the roller shutters being knocked four times stopped all thoughts and actions.

Billy looked at their faces, then whispered into her ear, "Now look at that babe, now that's fear, it's like the Devil himself has just knocked our front door."

"He probably is Billy so watch you lip, and don't aggravate this bloke!"

The guard dog barking blocked out the noise, as the company rottweiler attacked the outer door.

"JoJo," said Frank, "Go and put Ciril on a lease please, we don't want to upset the man before we even get to know him."

JoJo calmly walked out and through to the workshop he left the door open so that they could hear any conversation he had with the new visitor and tied the dog to the car ramp before opening the shutter doors for the new man.

Halfway up the man bent over and entered the workshop, he let the shutter rattle back down and locked it, "There, there, nice dog, you wouldn't bite a fellow mad dog, would you?" said the man as he looked at JoJo.

"He's a bit nasty, disturbing his afternoon nap is bad advice."

"Yes son, I know the feeling, and feel the same about my precious sleep being disturbed."

JoJo pointed to the doorway and walked off, followed by the new visitor who filled the doorway with his bulk as they waited for the Devil to enter the reception area.

He smiled at the crowd of people, "So, I answered a call, so who is the mouth in here?"

"That would be me sir," said Smith, Wayland Smith, level two, we worked together once."

The man grunted and looked at all the other faces, "So, give me the story so far then."

He stood in the doorway and gave them the impression of a Viking invader, the long greying hair and the moustache covering his top lip, but the shear bulk of him impressed them all.

"Mr Bloodworth?"

He stared into Smiths heart, "And who gave you, my name?"

"The office sir, and we have worked together, you searched for names, and I helped."

"Did you, ok, the bottom line please, I get bored really easily."

"Err ... we have acquired a great deal of money from the city of London stock exchange and require your services for protection of those who want it returned and quick."

"Thieves, you're just a bunch of thieve, anything else to add to this?"

"We stole the ghost dump from the city sir."

Mr Bloodworth refocused on the man speaking to him, "A ghost dump, so that would be a finance washing service, right?"

"Yes sir, from abroad."

"America, right?"

"Yes sir, the New York exchange services."

"Really?" he turned to leave, "You'll have to excuse me gents, this is not my type of job you understand, so I need to get a handle on what you players have done."

Sandra screeched out at them, "You useless fuckers, you try to scam the man who has your lives in his hands, you stupid fucking useless bastards!"

Mr Bloodworth focused on her and listened to her words, "And you are involved in all this?"

"They stole 120 billion pounds and put it into mine and Billy's account, so we are in the shit, and I am told that so are you, for even being here with us, they say that you are now compromised like the rest of us, I don't know about that, but just something to think about perhaps!"

"Hold on, so they have over one hundred, billion, pounds Stirling, correct?"

"Yes, 120 billions, stupid fuckers, eh?"

"Yes dear, there are other words for them, but you seem to have hit the nail on the head, stupid fuckers they are, and I'm now compromised?"

"They'll probably name you as the fixer, well, just look at em, they'll grass you up without saying a word and slide off to the sun."

"So, I'm compromised, eh? Not nice gentlemen, not nice at all, so you trapped me into this, not nice to be trapped, so who do I talk to around here then, the woman?"

"No, me!" said Billy, "The money is in my account and staying there until I'm satisfied of the job, they say you can do, we on the other hand don't know you, and could even think that you might have been with these fuckers all along, yes?"

"True, but I don't know these people, even the one over there who I know I have never worked with or for, so explain someone."

"Ten million for you and two million each for your men on completion," said Smith.

"I'm that cheap, am, so two billion would be a better price and a bill each for the boys?"

"Piss off, you're taking the piss now!" screeched Sandra.

"Four billion pounds Stirling, one as a starter and three on completion of the task!" said Billy.

"Billy!" screeched Sandra again, "We can't trust him we don't know him, do we?"

Billy thumbed to the gents still sitting and watching them, "And we can trust these bods, Sand? Now shut up and let me do this please darling."

Mr Bloodworth stared him down as he calculated the lads will to see this through.

"I have to assume that you have the balls for this kind of job young man?"

"Well, the game as you call it has found me so I must step up to the plate, right?"

"Yes, right! You'll need balls for this and what is going to happen son, so no, just two hundred grand for now and the pot on completion, clear so far?"

"A direct transfer to any bank of your choosing Mr Blood." said Sandra.

"Bloodworth dear, an old Viking name, I'm from a land up north, Yorkshire, have you heard of the county?"

"Sorry Mr Bloodworth."

"It's ok Sandra, all to be expected on our introduction, and not the first to get my name wrong, so, I have to add a disclaimer her people, and it is this, if any of my people are trapped, hurt or killed by anyone in this room then that person will feel my full wrath of vengeance, too scary you think Sandra?"

"No, I agree!"

"So how is this going to happen then?"

"Well, these dicks have stolen the money, so we have to assume they have a route for distribution," said Sandra,

"So, through me and Sandra only, Mr Bloodworth, we split equably when the time comes, no cheats and no bandits, yes?" said Billy.

"Fair play young man, and I agree, you must all know that I will not be cheated, ok, let me be clear here people, the little lady has rescued your scam from the flames of this fire, and I am fully determined to collect the full amount I am owed on completion, any questions so far?"

"So, who's plan do we follow?" asked Gerald.

Mr Bloodworth looked around for any ideas, but gave up and sniffed, "Ok, for now I will put you all on ice in one of my safe houses and well out of the way, your slate is clean so far, but any changes to your plan involving me and mine had better come forth at some time in the future, so I don't need names at this moment but I would like an idea on how the scam happens and what is expected from the losers of the money, any clues here?"

Gerald coughed to be heard, "Thank you Mr Bloodworth, for joining us, but as you can see, we are at an impasse, the young man has the money and also has the power, so we don't know how good or bad he can be."

Mr Bloodworth focused on Gerald, "And your boys have done the stealing and given it to a cockney thug, she's right about you, you lot are fucking greedy morons, you didn't expect him did you, so any suggestions of using violence to achieve your aims here?"

A sudden clank brought them around to observe Frank slam a sawn-off shotgun on his trade counter, he waited for their full attention, "Now, hold it right there, these are my people, my family as good as, and I will kill anyone trying the strong-arm stuff, I don't give shit who the hell you are fat boy!"

"Easy Frank." said Mr Bloodworth, he smiled at Frank in a familiar way.

"Do I know you then matey?"

"You don't remember me do you Frank? I worked for big Jim down the west end for a while."

"One of his pet psychopath's then?"

"Na, just kid in the wrong slot, well something like that, you know how it goes, right?"

"A bullet boy?"

"Something like that Frank, anyway, I evolved from his influence and grabbed a new life."

"From prison, doing a life stretch?"

Mr Bloodworth nodded, "So is Jim still breathing free air?"

"Oh, yes, I remember you now, GBH with extreme violence, life without parole, so the big question is this, how the hell does that work?"

Mr Bloodworth smiled again, "Enlistment in a system of rehabilitation for her Majesty."

Frank now realized that he had asked a question too far, and his red face said it all, as Mr Bloodworth glared at him.

Frank did the zip his mouth mime and the padlock through his lips, he locked it then threw the key over his shoulder, before giving him a toothy grin.

Mr Bloodworth started laughing at him, "Thanks for that Frank, fully understood!"

"So, what's next?" asked Billy.

"Ok, listen up, I'm putting you all in one of my safe houses, nice and comfortable and more importantly safe from those who would like information, so no coms to the outside world, nothing, for our safety understood, and that's all of you!"

"And in the absence of a known plan I'm taking over."

"The transfer, ass wipe!" screeched Sandra.

Mr Bloodworth turned and smiled at her, "Do you know woman, I'm beginning to like you, it's the direct translation I like most, so what is it you want?"

"Ten bill, transferred into my account in a Swiss bank as agreed before you showed up."

"Calm, lady, I can do that for you, no probs," said Gerald as he brought his laptop to the counter and opened it up.

"Yes, I like it, and we can all see the system working, so no excuses on the other end of this transaction, right?" said Mr Bloodworth.

"Too, right!" said Sandra, "Come on smart arse, start tapping!"

Mr Bloodworth had to laugh again as he listened to her cockney banter.

Billy caught his eye and smiled, "Street trader, in her veins, generations of em."

"And not expected from these gentlemen, correct?"

Billy grinned and shook his head.

Gerald started his transfer as Sandra watched his every move, but Mr Bloodworth walked away to the side of the room and listened to his unseen earpiece.

"So, thank you for that Mr Blue, very interesting and I'm hooked on the deal, are you with me on this, good, inform the lads when we start, we have big challenges ahead of us, so inform and prepare, make the call for the roundup!"

He turned to the listeners and smiled, "Well, the start already, it seems that you have stolen American money from some very dangerous people, and as a result they are sending one of their best hunter to find recover and destroy whoever you are, so the world is about to his us, they send a noted bounty hunter no less, a Mr John Winstanley, he lives in the UK, so he becomes handy for their search, I am told that he is meeting a banker from New York, called Bobby Vigo, anyone know this man?"

Gerald smiled at him but said nothing.

"So, you do then?"

"He's New York Mafia sir, and has links here in the UK, I am told that he owns people."

"Like a good Mafioso should, eh? So, do you know the family who back him?"

Gerald shook his head.

"So, this is how fast things can move when so much money is in the mix, you are lucky because they feel it was an inside job by traders on the banking floor."

He waited for Gerald to say something else, but he didn't, "So that would be your link then?"

"Our brother, Max, and the one who spotted the finance being ring fenced for American allotment procedures."

"Gobbledygook, and I'm supposed to understand that?"

"Banking terms sir, nothing more."

Mr Bloodworth scowled at him with obvious distain, "Bloody bankers, the blood sucking low life's of our society."

"Transfer!" screeched Sandra, "Come on, bloody get a move on."

Mr Bloodworth had to laugh again, "So, I'll gain more information from this Bobby Vigo and real them in with misinformation to divert their interests, anyone have another plan in mind before we transfer it all out?"

Billy gave him the stare, "You could sell us out to the Yank, no problem, and make a tidy sum for your retirement, but the downside of that is that they know you and your links, well, if it were me, I would be thinking about your links, and even run with the idea that this was always your plan, with you being a big player and all that?"

Mr Bloodworth turned to him and smiled, "Had time to think it through then lad, and as sharp as a tack, so what else have you got in that sparked up brain of yours?"

"They'll come over with the very attractive deal and offer retirement money, well it's a big old loss, right, but, and there's a great big but in there, you see, from their point of view, this shouldn't have happened, someone in the mix is a thief, you, me, them, everyone, and so you will be put to the sword, well, in the end, do you see that Mr Bloodworth?"

"And you have more to add to that alarm there, son?"

"And they must be shit scared of being on your playground, with your reputation of savagery, correct?"

"Not a word I use, but I can see where you're coming from on that, but what next then?"

"However, Mr Bloodworth, that can come in handy, you can get close to the owners, so close that you can?"

"Can what? Spit it out son!"

"Kill them!"

"Billy!" screeched Sandra.

"What, has no one thought this through enough, answer me this then, you bunch of smart arses, will they ever, forgive, walk away and forget, will we ever be forgiven, will we ever feel safe again?" No, we will be running for the rest of our lives, and that's including you Mr Bloodworth, run rabbit, rabbit run, forever, get it?"

"All of them? You mean go over there and kill a complete Mafia family, are you completely off your head son?" said Mr Bloodworth.

"He might not have the balls for this one Billy?" said Frank, still leaning on his counter.

"What the hell's wrong with you people this far east in London, what is it, a stronger pollution zone or something?" said Mr Bloodworth, he walked back over to Frank, "Does he not realize how hard it could be to kill them all?"

"Like sheep, Thomas," Frank had remembered his first name, "And just like sheep when under threat, they flock together, the trick is to get them to flock, get it?"

"And to do that we, what?"

"Wipe away their known office, paperwork, people, safes, the lot!" said Billy.

"This idea is fucking crazy!"

"Forget it Billy, I don't think the big lad has the balls for all this, we might have to go alone after all."

Mr Bloodworth turned back to Frank and smiled, "Piggy in the middle faze one, eh?"

"I can assemble a crew if needed, after all Billy boy has the dosh to do any bloody thing, get it?"

"And cut me out of the deal?"

"Hey, you're supposed to be the big contractor for this kind of work, so contract or hit the road and wipe their arses, you know what's coming for us don't you, but we can turn this town into fort Knox if needed."

Mr Bloodworth smiled again, "A good speech, and you would involve the dreaded west end?"

"Oh, no, never involve the west end, a very bad plan to begin with, no Jimmy the saw can sod off."

Mr Bloodworth pointed at him and smiled, "Good to see you keep in touch Frank."

"Look, Thomas, you can't sugar coat this one to your crew or even this bounty hunter, he's now in your boat and will be snuffed in time that very same as all of us who know their secret, bribe, bully, and blackmail the bastard to your will, and get the job done, clear?"

Mr Bloodworth had to burst out laughing again, "What the hell is this place?"

"We play on a smaller field than you Thomas, but we still know how to play the game, quick, ruthless and rapid action needed, cut the head from the body, no other way, well do you have another way than Billy's idea?"

Mr Bloodworth stopped laughing and stared at Billy, "And you have the balls for something like this?"

"I don't have a choice here, this is survival, for all of us, if you can come up with another plan then let's hear it?" said Billy, "That's the price of this payday, blood and lots of it!"

"My God, what a bunch of monsters we have here?"

"As Frank has just said, we have to bribe this Winstanley bloke, a big payday for all involved, I can give him a bill, yes?"

Smith coughed to lighten the mood a little, "Well if this is a crime family then we have help, because they will have enemies and we be the kingmakers if needed."

"Wow!" said Mr Bloodworth, "So you really are SIS, to come up with something like that."

"We use every lead, every friend in need, and besides, with a war rolling they might leave us alone and fight amongst themselves?"

"Yes," said Billy, "I like that angle, smoke and mirrors for the outside, poor old Mafia bosses won't know what hit em!"

"Let me think on that please."

"Yes, but you must agree on the outcome, no other way, right?"

Mr Bloodworth turned on him again, "And I thought today would be a clam day, and now this."

"Well?" screamed Sandra.

"Yes, agreed, and it will be done!"

"And I'll come along then?" said Billy.

"Billy!" screamed Sandra again, "You're a bloody civilian, he's the pro, so shut your trap because you ain't going right?"

"Agreed boy, you are not needed."

"Hold up, I'm paying for all this, so I want to be there."

"Billy!" she screamed.

"Sand, what if he comes back, oh yes folks, all gone, and then he's wrong and there are a few Mafia boys to chop us to pieces at leisure, then what, wise bloody up woman, I have to do this!"

"The trust issue again?"

"Yes, I trust him, but I want to see the evidence, understood?"

"He's right Billy, you are fucking bonkers!"

Mr Bloodworth was fascinated at witnessing the domestic in front of him, "But you might be killed in any action, do we still get paid?"

Billy turned to her and waited for her answer.

"Yes, but I'll be bastard fuming with your lot for incompetence, to lose the payer, that smacks of stupidity!"

"Calm woman!" said Mr Bloodworth, "He can be a driver, that's it, out of the action, just the taxi to and from, no problems and no worries, alright with that?"

"No, I bloody am not, but that's him, as thick as a brick!"

"It's just logic Sand, he could tell us anything and we'd believe him, but this is life and death, understood woman?"

"I'll try not to be insulted by this conversation kids." said Mr Bloodworth as he chuckled.

"And Mr Smith can get us information about the targets, if we need them."

"As if he ever worked in the Whitehall directorate, that is?" said Mr Bloodworth.

"I did twenty years and all I got was a clock and a warm boot up the arse."

"And that's how you blagged your way into this scam then?"

"What, he's not real?" screeched Sandra.

"Oh, he's real enough, but just not as informed as we would like and certainly not in the know of our targets, are you Wayland?"

"I have links, and I can ask friends."

"Well, he's in, so we ask when we need and see how good he is then," said Billy, "But first and not forgotten, we need that transfer!"

"Yes arsehole, get to the squiggles!" screeched Sandra.

Gerald grinned as he passed over the laptop for Billy to sign, "Both account holders please, just squiggle as you say, and within the blacked-out boxes."

"My grandads name?"

"Yes, yours, your grandads and Billys name, or these people will lose it on purpose, understood?"

"What, you or the Swiss?"

"I do not trust the cold hearted, cold handshake and cold smile of the Swiss!"

"But we have to trust you?"

Check it with your phone dear, the new account totals, the number is there on the screen."

She growled at him but signed it and passed over the plastic pen for Billy to do his signature.

"And both needed dear for any transfers, clear so far?"

She ignored him as she walked away and checked it with her phone, "Yes, done, thanks Geraldo!"

"Wow that was quick." said Billy.

"Well, you wanted a demo, and there you have it, ok, people?"

"Yes, thanks Gerald." said Billy, "But Sand, how the hell did you remember the numbers?"

"Shut up, you tart, who does the numbers around here, me!"

Mr Bloodworth walked back over to Frank to ask another question, "So, do you still contact Jim now and again?"

"Why, do you need his help?"

"No, I have my own systems and his is, well, is savage, right?"

"Oh, yes, old Jim is a savage, but can you do this away game?"

Mr Bloodworth smiled, "Not convinced of my abilities?"

"Na, just curious, so keep your knickers on."

"I will, and I owe Jim a visit as well."

"Funny, that's, because so do I, Thomas, one thing I do know though and that is, on this one you're going to have to earn your corn walking in blood."

"That's my name after all Frank."

"Just make the yanks earn their corn, push for help but do not trust as you would a Brit, clear?"

"An old man's advice?"

"From experience Thomas, so listen up, and don't be a smart arse with em!"

"Thanks for the advice dad."

"And don't take the piss with the kid, he's as smart as any of your lot, so give him respect and listen if he comes up with an alternative plan, because he will, so keep on your toes with him."

Mr Bloodworth had to laugh at the old man's instructions, "Or what?"

"Look smart arse without talent it all falls to rat shit, now you know that one, don't you, I bet it was one of Jims plans that did for you, and your ten stretch, correct?"

Mr Bloodworth nodded and smiled at him, "You too, eh?"

Frank nodded back to him in silence.

"Could be times to make amends, don't you think?"

"Could be old man!"

CHAPTER 5 ... FLAT... SOUTH KENSINGTON ... LONDON.

Ned unlocked Mr Simperates front door and walked in, Max followed on and sniffed the air.

"What the hell is that smell?"

Ned pointed to the little dog now in front of them, "A jack Russell, just a pup, so he must be the guard dog."

"Oh, shut up and lets just get this done."

Max walked off to plant his supposed evidence around the flat, but the dog took a liking to Ned's shoes and followed him around trying to bite them, so he walked into the kitchenet and found a plastic container with dog food in it, he opened the lid and placed it on the floor.

"What, too boring right?"

The little dog looked at him and then the food but didn't want to eat.

"Yes boy, I'd be the same," He walked over to the fridge and opened the door to search for something the dog could eat, "Sausages, good enough for you boy?"

He ripped open the packet and dropped the lot on the floor, the dog started scoffing at speed.

"New to all this good grub eh, boy?"

Max, removed a picture from the wall and placed it on the desktop, then took a cuckoo clock out of his bag and placed it on the wall in the spot, "Looks good, eh Ned, the man has obviously travelled all over."

He opened the desk draw and dropped in an old Swiss watch and some small change together with a few Swiss francs to add to the man's guilt.

He rummaged around to find a notebook then put it in his pocket and replaced it with one of his own he had previously doctored for this occasion.

"What's that?" asked Ned.

"Oh, just a few incriminating notes from friends in the banking system in his favorite holiday spot on the slopes, he loves all that you know."

"Does he?"

"Oh, yes, a girl in every café and bar, a bit of a slosher really."

"Is he?"

"Oh, yes, hey you can't give a pack of sausages to a pup, it'll make him sick."

"Oh, sorry boy!" Ned picked up the remains of the sausages and dropped them back in the fridge.

"Ok Mr Nedlington, lets rock and roll!"

"Yeah, but what about him?"

"Well. It's his dog, so what?"

"Well, if old Desperate is kept in after school, and gets his arse slapped pink, then this poor little man will starve, now that can't be right, can it?"

"Yeah, I suppose so, ok, we'll leave the door open, and he can find a new home around here."

"Yes, and then gets run over by a flash car in the street."

"Ah, ok, give him to someone on the way, after all he's a lovable little guy."

"Or we could have him?"

"Ned, you can't steal the man's dog mate, now that's just not right, is it?"

"And all this isn't?"

"Ah, you have me there, ok, just let's go and meet up at the garage."

"Garage?"

"The mechanic, the man with all our dosh?"

"Ah, yes and the big cheque book?"

"That's the very man, I just hope he can spell."

CHAPTER 6 ... FRANK WARREN CARS.

The driver of the minibus parked outside pressed his earpiece, "Two men and a little dog approaching boss, oh, and another dog wanting entry to the garage, could be a stray, the men are young, not locals, far too smart to be locals, knocking now, out!"

Mr Bloodworth touched his ear again, "Thank you Mr Blue, friends I think, keep tabs on any nosey neighbors please, intercept if needed, we need silence for a moment before we come out and load the bus."

He turned to the faces as the door shutter knocked, the Rottweiler reacted to the noise by barking again.

Frank nodded to the young apprentice, "Calm Ciril down will you JoJo, and let them in, friends, right gentlemen?"

"My brother Max and Ned, his friend, these are the people who did the transfer in the first place." said Gerald.

They watched the two men walk in; Ned was holding the Jack Russell pup in his arms as another dog pushed his way through their legs to greet Frank behind the counter.

"Oh, this is Albert, a classic London stray, he sleeps in the park and eats here most days, a good life if you can get it."

"Put the dog down son, he has to learn the skills."

"What skills?"

"The how to be a dog skills, watch and learn dog sociability in action."

Ned placed the little dog on the floor and Albert immediately stood over him and sniffed.

"Take him into the workshop and let Ciril have a sniff of him and see how diplomacy can work with a new stranger, we could all learn a great deal from dogs you know."

Ned looked at the man speaking to him, but Gerald gave him the news, "This is Frank, as in Frank Warren cars, and that man over there is William Boncour, the man you sent the money to gents."

Max looked around the faces, "And the money?"

"Oh, he's quick!" said Sandra.

Billy grinned at them, "Yes, thanks chaps, mine of course, very nice of you, shocking at first but now I have the handle of the whole thing."

"Max looked to his brothers, "But?"

"Yes lad, some very big buts in here!" said Mr Bloodworth

The two literally, had to looked up to the man in front of them.

Mr Bloodworth smiled at the new arrival's, "You see the deal has been done on your behalf, so I'm placing you under Franks protection until the dreaded work is complete, your friends and family will explain it all at a later date."

"Thanks Thomas, I'll have the dog as well, a fine poaching pair, and a trigger for a dozy Rotty, the little lad won't let him sleep if he hears something, again, we could all learn from these animal."

Ned's face dropped, in sudden sadness.

"Oh, give it a rest Ned!" said Max.

"Well, Frank, any good for you in times of need?" Mr Bloodworth nodded to the two new young arrivals.

"Like puffters."

"Most of them are these days old man."

"For what?" asked Billy.

"Bluff and bluster young man, that's all, just to stand and be mean looking if needed."

"There have been some changes to the original plan Max, and Mr Bloodworth has taken control of the planning for our safety and Billy over there has taken over the money, we are now useful servant when needed." said Gerald.

"But with the same cut?" asked Max.

"Yes!", said Billy, "But you still have to work for it, that's all, and no risk in your case, just fill ins now and again ok, with all that?"

"No, not really, I had a code ready and waiting for the transfer."

"And leaving us to pay the bills, eh?" said Sandra.

Gerald nodded to her, "And the wife of the said William Boncour, Sandra Boncour, the new money madam."

"You make it sound like I'm on the game Geraldo?"

"Well, you are now, aren't you darling."

She returned to her stop right there, stare and silenced any other comment.

"But I have people waiting!" said Max.

"One week, and it will be all bing, band, bosh!" said Billy, "Best ask your brothers for the full plan layout, but in your own time please, because we're now on a time limit, clear so far?"

Max shook his head in total confusion.

"So, you completed program B?" asked Gerald."

"Err yeah, that's his dog out there, so he looks like the culprit all along."

"Good, and your ex-boss?"

"Needs a clean shirt." said Ned.

Gerald asked with his eyes and Max answered.

"A bit of an accident in the office, damn useless coffee machines!"

"Good, look gents, we have been given some reality from the fallout from all this and feel as a group that we should follow the experience and listen to Mr Bloodworth, understood?"

"So can this man give anything away about you and your friend here?" asked Mr Bloodworth.

"Numbers and addresses, that's it I suppose."

"So how long do you think it will take to get on your trail?"

"Oh 24 hours maximum."

"Wrong young man, the big bunce is on the plain heading this way as we speak, and together with a bounty hunter based here in the UK he will be here in a matter of hours."

"No way, no chance!"

"Yes chance, so listen up, everyone get in the mini bus and Mr Blue will take you to a nice warm out of the way building to hide in, my bolt hole in the woods, and now if any of you contact the outside world and bring hunters down on us I will blame that man accordingly, I'll let the people who've listened to my speech pass it on the news to the newcomers, clear so far people?"

"But I have plans rolling?" said Max

"Now look kid, this has got very serious, you see the new plan is this, we go over to America and kill them all, now could the plan be simpler?" said Mr Bloodworth.

Gerald pinched Max to shut him up and whispered in his ear, "We'll take later, we just need to descale the originals and plan a loan stage agreement for your clients."

Max stared at them open mouthed.

"The new plan is going to be bloody, clear?" said Billy, "New plans are like that."

"But we were just going to get lost!" said Ned.

"And be hunted down and skinned alive, so we have a brand-new plan, clear?" said Billy.

"Bring the minibus round Mr Blue, we are about to load up." said Mr Bloodworth in his earpiece.

Billy gave him his best smile, "So, you accept my new plan, lock stock and smoking barrel's?"

"With reservations young man."

"Such as?"

"Well, the fact that you have a big mouth and could cause more trouble than you're worth."

"Yes, but I'm the paymaster, I have the right."

"Let me think on that for a moment."

"And the meet with the hunter, now that could be interesting, I think."

"No!"

"But I'm the payer, I have the right."

"For a good slap if you don't shut up and get in the bus!"

Sandra pulled his sleeve and dragged him to the minibus, "Get in and shut up Billy."

"Yes babe, but it's me who makes the deal and not him."

Mr Bloodworth looked at Frank, "So, rear guard, just in case Frank?"

"If they want me then they'll have to pay in pain, I still have local friends in the business you know Thomas, this is my manor, so I don't need your lock up, understand?"

"But these are nasty folk Frank, they don't play by the rules."

"And nor do I if needed Thomas."

He nodded to Frank and smiled, "Do it your own way old man, but you know the rules, right?"

"I wrote most of them sonny! You just make damn sure the golden boy is not harmed in any way, he is more valuable than you, get me?"

"Is he that good?"

"My problem solver, it's the ice-cold logical thinking, he sees it as it is, now that's hard for us sometimes, right?"

Mr Bloodworth looked at him for a second or two before smiling at him, and ushering people out to the minibus.

CHAPTER 7 ... HEATHROW AIRPORT ... ARRIVALS LOUNGE.

John Winstanley hoped he could recognize the face of Bobbt Vigo, he had met him once in New York and knew he was connected to the mob on the west side, and he was a problem because he could pass on valuable information to his bosses, and John didn't want them to know about him and his work in the UK.

He shuffled around with his cardboard sign that read, New York Investments.

He needn't have worried because Bobby Vigo spotted him first and shouted down the customs hall to him.

"Hi John, with you in a moment, over here man!"

John waved back and waited until the customs man gave him the nod to go out of the building, John looked at him through the plastic-glass wall and worried about the job in hand.

They shook hands at the exit doors, "A good flight Bobby?"

"No, not a good flight, look, this is strictly business, so let's get this done because my neck is on the line with this little fiasco!"

"Welcome to the UK Bobby, cheer up man, this is easy street."

"Not in my book John."

Winstanley's phone burst into action so he pressed green and listened to the massage recording.

"Wow, done and dusted, now that has to be a record somewhere don't you thin Bobby boy?"

"What is?"

"I have them, the whole kit and caboodle, money and villain's all waiting for us to converse and find out the who, the where, and the when, cool ha?"

"Is it, so where do we go?"

Bobby followed on with his little overnight case and watched where Winstanley was looking.

He turned to Bobby, "Ok, that's one of his guys in the Jag, now listen up very carefully, this is their patch, and they are very aggressive if spooked, get me?"

"What is it you're saying John?"

"My friend over here Thomas Bloodworth has them in his lockup, cool, eh?"

"Wow that is very cool John, and the money?"

"Only a matter of time Bobby and we'll have it all, so how much did they steal?"

Bobby looked around for listening ears, then whispered, "Over a hundred billion and that's in pounds John, understood how it will go in the States if I fail on recovery on this one?"

"And my fee?"

"A hundred big ones, and no questions asked, ok, with that?"

"Was that ten percent you were talking about Bobby?"

"Shit, I can't give that much away man."

"Ten per are the rules of any contract here Bobby, agree or I walk, understand me?"

"Ok, agreed, just get the money back and I can get out of this shit country fast."

John walked up to the Jaguar and shook hands with the driver, "Mr Red at your disposal sir, to your hotel I assume?"

Bobby watched the man closely, the smart suit the red tie and the shiny shoes.

"Just call me John Mr Red." He opened the rear door for Bobby to climb in and Mr Red got in the driver's seat and waited for them to say they were comfortable.

John nodded to him in the mirror and the car pulled off into the traffic, he held Bobby's knee and whispered to him to keep his mouth shut and not to talk shop in any way.

He continued to whisper in his ear, "Now listen up, Thomas Bloodworth runs a system over here who get rid of unwanted or troublesome people, he has a system of colors, Mr Red here is one of his boys and this is a curtesy ride into London, a favor you see, because he wants my help in the states on another matter, clear so far?"

Mr Red coughed in the driver's seat and looked at them in the interior mirror, "Mr Black would like a word in your shell-like sir, so I'm taking you to the park, ok?"

Bobby elbowed John, "What the hell does that mean?"

"They seem to speak English, but they don't, shell- like is your ear, he wants a word or three, cockney banter they call it, understood?"

"Not really John, so why the meeting, and who is Mr Black?"

"Thomas Bloodworth, that's his call sign and coded words have to include their color."

"Colors!"

"Yes sir, colors, I am Mr Red, and you are about to meet Mr Black," said Mr Red.

John squeezed his knee to shut up, "Listen, Mr Black runs a tight ship, so let me ask, ok?"

Bobby was confused but became silent.

"Ok Mr Red, now just for us foreigners in fact, and it goes no further here, could you tell us how you came to be in Mr Blacks employ?"

"Not allowed sir."

John leaned forward and touched Mr Reds shoulder, "Just for us guy, to get a handle of who and what we're up against over here."

Mr Red grinned into the mirror again, "Well, by trade I'm a brick layer and finishing a contract my boss refused to pay me what he owed me, so anyway, I got really mad and buried him alive in his own cement mix, they called it extreme GBH with violent intent and I was banged up for life."

"That's grievous bodily harm Bobby, with intention to kill, or murder one as we call it, clear?"

"So anyway, I was doing time when an animal called Mr Black sprung me to a life of service, and here I am, I signed the pink and serve the crown in complete silence, ok with that?"

"What the hell is this, John?"

"Shush, his Mr Black, that's our Mr Bloodworth runs this program, now listen up again, so Mr Red, to your knowledge has anyone in memory, say ever done him wrong and survived?"

"You won't say anything of this to him will you sir?"

"No Mr Red, zip baby!"

"So, the answer to your question is this, no, none, any deserters, failures or arseholes find a shallow grave or float down the river Thames toot sweet, clear so far sir?"

"Shit!" said Bobby, "And we deal with these people?"

"The world deals with these people Bobby, so listen up again here, the meet must be about your bad news, so he's had a sniff of the amount lost, so follow me and say nothing to his face, just let me do the talking, ok?"

"Err ... yes John, all yours!"

"He'll want a slice, Bobby."

"Yes, but what kind of name is that, Blood?"

"Be respectful Bobby, this is England, and different rules apply, so the money?"

"Yes, ok, do it, just get it done so I can go home from this suicide mission."

"He's from up north where they all have these strange names, Viking names he tells me, and they're all very aggressive if it goes wrong, you understand, so shtum, please! You'll understand when you meet the man."

Mr Red in the driver's seat gave out a little giggle before turning into Horse Guards and pulling to a stop, to let his customers out onto the grass.

"The big man in the middle, you can't miss him sir!" said Mr Red with a smile.

John held his hand out to shake Mr Blacks hand who shook it and smiled.

"Welcome to England John."

"Err ...Thomas, this is Mr Vigo from the States, he's the one with the problems."

"Yes John, understood, so did you explain the deal to him?"

"Yes Thomas, but as you know, these bankers are as tight as a duck assess man!"

"We'll pay Mr Black, ten percent I assume, the same as John here, right? Just do it, because my ass is on the line here!"

He smiled at the Americans before speaking again, "Ah, a slight change of plan here lads, you see I have been offered a second contract and a greater amount than you can ever offer, with a twisted safety feature to boot."

"What does that mean Thomas?"

"It means that I want to complete the contract and so do my colors!"

"What the hell is this, John?" squeaked Bobby.

"Shush Bobby, let's just hear the man out."

"Ok, hear me out please before you make any decisions, so how has this settled in the States, Mr Vigo?"

"Panic is the word and crazy is the attitude."

"Ok, and so if the money and the thieves are located and put down, then what?"

"I don't know what you mean sir?"

"What are you saying Thomas?" asked Winstanley.

"Answer me this simple question, so all's calm, money back in their bank, then what?"

"Well, we go back to work as normal man!" said Bobby.

"No Bobby, I think I know what he's trying to say here, that the mob won't forget this and the people in the middle of it, he's saying that we will all get killed for being involved in their secret money laundering project over here in the UK, right Thomas?"

"Right John, we will all fall out of buildings or get run over in a tragic accident, all very sad but we'll all be snuffed, get it?"

"No, no, they won't do that, it'll be business as normal, it'll be sweet I promise man!"

"And his promise is worth what John?"

"Sand through his fingers Thomas, I get you man, we're in big trouble just being here and talking to you, man, Booby here has just dragged us into his pool man!"

"Exactly John!"

"So, your plan is what Thomas?"

"We cut the head off the snake, and we kill them all, the whole mob of them!"

"Shit!" squeaked Bobby.

But John burst out laughing, "You can't be serious man, there is maybe a hundred of them."

Mr Black stared him down into silence and he breathed in and out slowly.

"My God, you're serious man!"

"Yes, so that's the contract, and two billion is your share, because we need American help."

"Shit Thomas, you guys are stark raving crazy man!"

"This is going to happen, mark my words here John, I'll supply the full crew for the job, but we need inside information, understand? Jump in with an alternative plan of action if you have one John, I can change a plan, no problems."

"Shit, you're for real on this!"

"He's right though John," said Bobby, "If this gets out, they'll lose more than a ghost dump, this will destroy the markets, so yes, their plan will have to be silence all parties involved in this, I agree with him John."

"So, I'm point man then, in the States, right?"

"Yes, the point man as we clear up the mess for them."

"You're a fucking animal Thomas Bloodworth, what kind a name is that anyway?"

"The worth of blood, it's a Viking name, a present from my ancestors and I feel I need to live up to it, any objections? I feel that we can also be the revenge for all those lost souls in the drug empire these people run with fear and greed in mind."

"Yes Thomas, you live up to the name, but just a thought twist if you like, so what about employing sub-contractors, and obviously they would bite the dust on completion, not to your British sensibilities?"

"Shit, you guys are monsters!" screeched Bobby.

"Best not forget that one Bobby or you could end up a stain on the freeway."

Mr Bloodworth watched John eyes as he spoke and knew he would have to think again about their relationship for the future contract work, he smiled at John then turned, "Ok, here in the morning, say 06.00, for a final scheduling of the plan and small details to be agreed on, yes?"

"Yes Thomas, agreed!"

"I need a plan from your end, I need to know about the crime families in New York, the who's who, and where they stand with each other, in other words I need a killing slot, a time and a place that will affect them the most, and of course I need your bank details for your transfer, this boy is paying us all off on completion, understood?"

"Oh, and if you don't show, I'll hunt you down and kill you both, understand my business practice here John?"

"Yes Thomas, standard business practice is good for me as well."

Mr Bloodworth walked away in silence and disappeared into the crowd of Japanese tourists near the army barracks.

"Shit John, that guys crazy!" said Bobby.

"Yes Bobby, but soon to be very rich crazy, so we fall in line, understand?"

"Really?"

"We have no choice here Bobby, this is death or glory, in quick stages."

"But what do I do?"

"Well, you make the call and calm the waters over there, plenty of smiles and hand shaking, we've won, haven't we?"

"Shit!" screeched Bobby, his face was white with fear.

"Yes, you make the call when we get to the hotel and make it easy and sorted, bada bing, bada bang, clear?"

Mr Bloodworth picked up his phone and made another call, "Mr White, a general recall please, we have a contract we need to fulfill."

"Sir, and the location required."

"Water, Graves End, Kent, I feel it's the right place for this gathering, all the current colors please, any about to join us?"

"No sir, some are still in the training stage."

"Good, keep on top of them as usual and meet me there, what time is dawn tomorrow?"

"Err.... just searching, that's 03.34 sir."

"Good, that's the assembly time then and be smart please, this is official, clear the calendar please, this is priority."

"But we have a Government contract obligation?"

"Scrub that, we have priorities on the line, inform Mr White of the new schedule, clear?"

"Clear sir!"

CHAPTER 8 ... GRAVES END ... MUD FLATS ... TIDAL ESTUARY.

Mr Black welcomed them all with a wave and a smile as they assembled, "Looking good kids, but are you really?"

The faces of his team looked at him with excitement and surprise at the venue and time.

"I called an early call because I have a busy schedule today, so strip down gentlemen because we're going for a swim."

The early morning mist hung over the estuary as they all started to take off their clothes.

As he undressed, he spoke to them, "Now I hope you have cancelled all appointments and jobs for the next two week, I also hope that you have registered your bank details into the system for payments for when this contract is concluded, if not then you are doing this for free, and you're an idiot!"

The laughing started as they listened.

"We have a full dance card of a contract, so I need brains and guts in that order, so we swim, goggles on, and we swim to that floating dock over there in the estuary, any who fail to arrive because they drown will be laughed at by the rest of us for being morons for not keeping up the fitness regime, we are an immediate action group after all, clear so far, ok, go!"

The splashes started as one by one they waded through the mud to the water and swam off.

He stopped and faced Mr White, "Not you son, you are the chosen man, I now formally hand over all responsibilities and ties to the colors over to you, yours to train and bring on to my standard, clear?"

Mr White shook his head in disbelief, "No, not bloody clear!"

"You now have the system, because all of us are now retired from service, and if we meet again, I will expect to be killed by you or one of yours, because?"

"You'll be working for another system! Anyway, you'll understand when you read the headlines coming from the States."

"You boy, we're done as of now, understood?" Mr Black turned away and waded away into the mud and eventually swam away into the sea mist.

"Bastard!" screamed Mr White, "Not bastard clear boss, this is not right!"

The giggling and screeching continued as they swam away to the middle of the estuary, some reached the floating pontoon faster than others and a game started when some pushed the others back in, just for fun.

Suddenly the game stopped as Mr Black straightened up and smiled at them.

"Now, I've tried to kill you all as individuals at one time or another during your training, but here you are, killers all, yet survivors of the colors program, and I would be surprised if you lot didn't have your primary weapon on you, yes?"

He looked around the assembled colors and spotted the odd one or two with their Sikes number one pattern stiletto in the teeth, others held up their dagger to show him he was right.

"Mr Green, you seem to be an animal sir!"

The laughter echoed over the estuary, as he conducted the brief.

"Ok, listen up, because this is the big one, the retirement one, the one we have all been waiting for, after this, you uglies will disperse and be gone from each other's lives, because if we meet again after this, then we will kill that man because ......?"

"He'll be working for another system!" they said in unison.

"And personal safety is all, because ....?"

"We live the life; so, we pay the price!" echoed over the water as they shouted in unison again.

"Good, ok, the job is this, we are going to America, and we are going to wipe out a complete Mafia family, total annihilation of all bad guys, clear all?"

They rumbled in expected gossip and as he stared at them, "Ok, calm all, and the pay is one, billion pounds each, I repeat myself for the cloth ears among us, that's one billion pounds each, paid on completion of the said contract, any questions?"

He shut them up with a fierce stare," Ok, so, before you start ordering your super cars, let me just say this, the job is going to be bloody, we kill them all, and that main part of the contract clause, total annihilation, clear?"

"And secondly, this is going to happen in New York City, the big apple as they call it, for us though, we're killing the pips!"

They laughed but it wasn't funny.

"Ok, I need a burglar for a little side issue, oh, well done Mr Green, for volunteering for that mission, and no sticky finger please, this is business."

The others laughed at his face.

"I need a planner, and that's you Mr Blue and support crew, that's you Mr Red, so the rest of you killers hold fast for the call and the quick action require at that time, you will be informed when and if, because the important part is ....?"

"To be ready!" the unified shout echoed over the water.

Mr Black thought of the disappointed Mr White but then thought about their escape if everything went wrong.

"Ok, and rule one applies, a call for everyone for himself is the last call I make, and you lot spilt accordingly because that means that the contract is aborted and lost, not words I wish to give out or even hear, understood?"

"Right, put on the overalls over there in the box and then climb into the boat.

They looked around for a boat, then spotted the half rib attached to the pontoon, some pointed and giggled at the twin engines and knew it was going to be the ride of their lives.

"I never really liked you lot, but you are brethren and are bonded to me in our blood ties as I am to you, you may smell and be as ugly as sin, but you are brethren and so ....?

"I save your life, as you save mine!" shouted the group with the long taught and remembered mantra, the sound was louder as it echoed down the estuary.

He jumped into the driver's seat of the marine rescue half rib and smiled and counted them in as they climbed aboard, "I want you to be American footballers returning home at the airport, you will be gone on site, do not speak to the Americans, just hang around and go on their flight, to be met by Mr Driver, at JFK, he will supply the tools of your trade, he is also a contractor and works for me, ask for nothing else, and keep to the codes, or I will ....?

"Beat the crap out of us!" they screeched as one, then started laughing as the mad man started up the engines and blasted off into the ocean and down the coast, they watched him grin into the wind as his long hair was blown dry, and it was as if he were a Viking invader, searching for a prize, they all knew that he really was.

Some tried to hum a Viking song from the tv series, but it was all too bouncy in the rising surf of the incoming tide.

Mr Black whispered into the cold wind after he had pressed the hammers down, "This will be my last Lord Odin, give us luck in battle for this last one, please!"

The lads clung on for dear life in excitement to be involved in a contract at last.

They whooped as he blasted the boat down the coast to a landing stage, where other clothes awaited them, now they were New York Jets, on tour.

"Behave gentlemen because if you don't behave, I will ....?

"Beat the cap out of us!" they screamed and laughed with him.

"No smart arses, no arguing, no fights, Mr Brown is number one until we meet up for the kill, you will obey his orders, or I will ....?

"Beat the cap out of us!" they screamed at him.

He pointed to the minibus at the side of the road, "I'll see you in New York, so be ready, or?"

"You'll beat the crap out of us!"

He gave them the clenched fist razed in the air, hand signal for being aware at all times, then walked off in silence, letting them get dressed in the track suits provided, he got into a Land Rover and drove off, leaving them in a cloud of diesel fumes.

Mr Red looked into the eyes of Mr Blue, "Well?"

"Well, what?"

"Well, what are you buying first?"

The group laughed together hearing their conversation, brethren all, and all for one.

CHAPTER 9 ... BANK OF ENGLAND ... AMERICAN EXCHANGE.

John Winstanley closed the door to the office and made sure no one was listening to their conversation, "So, ready?"

Bobby Vigo was so very nervous, so he drank a Scotch and water straight back in one gulp, then burped, "Ok, this has to be casual, and calm, so be calm."

"Relax Bobby, nice and relaxed, you're just informing them of our great success over here in London, be cool and calm, ok, with that?"

He punched in the New York number and pressed for the call, then waited for the pickup.

"Hello!" came the deep dark American voice on the other end of the line.

"Hello Danny, it's Bobby Vigo over the pond in London, so everything is cool and on schedule."

"Really, Bobby, well done guy, I knew you could do this, we had full faith in your skill, so who was it?"

"Oh, just a London crew, too big for their boots, greedy you see, but anyway we have them and the money so no sweat, a friend of mine, and one of our private contractors helped with his English sub-contractor, they're really good guys, it all dove tailed nice and easy."

"Well perhaps a long vacation is in order, the Don is in Florida, so come and visit, we can have a great time, fishing, eating good food, and drinking the best wine in our country, bring the guys along Bobby, we can all celebrate and have fun, yes?"

"Oh, yes Danny, these guys would love all that."

"Ok, that's a date then, give me a call when you hit the States, we have a great deal to discuss about you and your promotion, get me Bobby boy?"

"Yes Danny, and thanks for all this."

"My pleasure Bobby, looking forward to having a shindig and drinks with you guys! Oh, I've just had a thought here Bobby, so did you get a name for these London people?"

"Err ... no Danny, but they were connected, and it was an inside job as you said it would be."

"Oh, good, we'll discuss it later, right?"

"Yeah Danny, see ya later!" he closed the call and took a couple of deep breaths.

John Winstanley poured him another Scotch, but straight up and passed it over to him over the table.

"Well done, Bobby, and was the sly convo invite to a party slipped into the conversation?"

"Yes John, just as you said it would be."

"And your opinion on that special invitation to have a drinks is what?"

Booby put two fingers to his head and pulled the trigger.

"He's right then, we'll all be snuffed to make the coverup of the ghost dump?"

Bobby breathed out slowly and drank the whisky down in one.

"So, we're on then Bobby, so do you want to be involved in any of this?"

Bobby shook his head in shock at the question.

"Ok, Bobby, get dressed because we're on the town tonight."

"But John?"

"Look, he'll have people watching us as back up, understood? We have to behave like we've just won the world series because we have kid, so pull up the pants and let's go!"

"By the way John, the Don is in Florida, so how are you going to handle that one?"

CHAPTER 10 ... HEATHROW AIRPORT ... LONDON WEST.

The New York Jets had beaten their fellow American footballers at the Wembley stadium and at the airport they were all in high spirits, fooling around and buying fancy sunglasses at the shops.

Mr Black watched his boys mingle with the fellow track suits from a distance, but his colored men had seen him watching their every move and knew the consequence of making a hash of this send off to the contract, so they mingled together until the boarding call came over the Tannoy system, they walked and talked away to the boarding lounge.

He gave them the stare to get going and board early, "Because to be on time, one has to be early." He mumbled as he watched them walk off.

"And bloody behave or I'll slap you lot silly!"

They wheeled off with their cases and some gave him the hand signal for game on, the two fingers scratching the scalp.

"Just be gone and doing!" he growled under his breath as he watched.

He drove off and hoped all his training over the years of training was worth it and he wouldn't lose any of them because of bad luck and more importantly, bad planning.

His phone pinged on the dash, He pressed hands free and shouted, "Yes?"

"Oh, Mr Black, I've had a really good idea, do you want to hear it?" said Billy.

"Not at the moment, I'm coming to you, we'll talk within the hour, your new name by the way is Mr Grey, and that's what you will answer to and call yourself during this contract, clear?"

"Yeah, very, so I've come up with a plan."

"Yes, ok, look, I've got to be at a meet with Winstanley in an hour, in Hyde park, I'll talk to you afterwards, ok?"

"No, it's not ok, I want to be there!"

"No!"

"Hey, I'm paying for you little jolly over there and I want to see this bloke face up to judge if he's any good, understood?"

"Not the thing to do, he's not expecting another to be with me, he could get very funny, it's not the professional thing to do Billy so shut the fuck up!"

"Hey, I'm Mr Grey, one of your team and part of your security, nothing funny about that."

"You boy, are giving me a headache!"

"What time are you picking me up then boss?"

Mr Black so wanted to give this kid a good slap, but he had to laugh at his persistence.

"What time do you want me to be at Hyde park then, I'll get a cab?"

"Ok, squirt, 09.00 and to be on time one has to be......?"

"Early boss, yes, got it, see you in an hour, Speakers corner?"

"No, the center of the grass, and be bloody silent, and let me do the talking, not a fart, clear?"

"Yes boss, abso bloody and all that!"

Mr Black cut him off and regretted it, he's seen so many smart and eager kids like him killed and failed in their ambitions and wants, he'd seen hundreds of Billy's, during his life and didn't want to lose another one.

He breathed out and turned off the M25 and headed for central London, "And you had better be on time Winstanley, or you're out!" he grumbled.

CHAPTER 11 ... HYDE PARK ... CENTRAL LONDON.

John Winstanley was shocked to meet two people when he was only expecting to meet Mr Black, it showed in his face as they walked up to him.

"Relax John, just another bod in the colors, this is Mr Grey."

"Not professional Thomas and dangerous to change rules like this!" Billy stared into his eyes as he listened, then back to Mr Black.

Winstanley knew that the young man was a fake, he didn't fit in with Bloodworth's other bods as he called them, "You are bugging me Thomas, a new face to a meet, I don't know him, but what I do recognized about him, is that he is not one of yours, ease my concern and explain please!"

Mr Black turned on Mr Grey, "You see, spotted right off, get some understanding of the game now Mr Grey? Please excuse my rudeness John, but the man here is the payer of the contract, and he wanted to meet you, for his own stupid ideas, sorry."

Winstanley stared Billy down, "And he wants to be part of all this?"

"Yes!" said Billy, "But I'm here to see the job done so our retirement isn't disturbed by survivors, understood?"

Mr Black turned on him again, "Remember what I said back there Mr Grey, shut the fuck up!"

"Sorry John, so you have information for me?"

John looked from face to face and back again, "Well, as always, situation change, the old man has gone to his defended hacienda in the Florida keys, I'm told it's like an old-fashioned country estate, gate hoses, gun emplacement's, electronic surveillance in all four corners, so to cut it short Thomas, we're fucked!"

"There are always new ideas to crack a tin can Mr Winstanley!" said Billy.

"Is he for real here Thomas, and why would he want to be part of this slaughter?"

"He has a brain John, but his mouth is running too fast for it at the moment, he is the planner for this caper by the way, logical planning seems to be in his blood, now I can work with that, so patience please, bringing up new blood and all that."

"And he pays?"

"Oh, absolutely Mr Winstanley!" said Billy.

"Look Thomas, I have to give you the heads up on movement, the Don has started recruiting over here, not my department and supposedly not in my knowledge either, but he is, so what's spooked him do you think?"

"Money John, just lost money, so this could get really complicated, anything else?"

"Well New York is still there, and his main office is still working, so maybe start there?"

"Yes, I like the idea, so we are short of work tools, can you supply, if I start buying, they might get the impression I'm going to start a war or something, yes?"

"Yeah, not a problem, so what is it you need?"

"Ten of us, so two each, and shorts for all and longs MP 5's please, plus plenty of ammo with carrying pouches, oh, and the latest body armor, ceramic, if possible, would be good, and can you get hold of mines, smoke and claymores preferably?"

"A war zone then?"

"Just reserves, you never know do you?"

"So, he's got the wind up, I bet he's rang Jimmy the saw and asked for information, so that means that he doesn't trust you Mr Winstanley."

Winstanley stared at Mr Black, who just shrugged back at him.

"Natural talent, we have to let it go, don't you think John, the future is here they say."

Winstanley turned to Billy, "So you know Jimmy the saw then?"

"No, but my boss does, and so does Mr Black here, now that could be thrown into the mix to stir them up a bit eh, wouldn't that get the feathers flying?"

Winstanley focused on Billy again, "I might have to shoot him Thomas!"

"Me first!"

"I tell you what," said Billy, now getting into his planning ideas, "I'll get Sandra to spread a rumor on the net, something like, well subtle like, who's lost billions then, you know, taunt the bloke, wind him up, we could call the piece just Billions, people over here and even fellow families over there are obviously laughing at him, right? So, he'll get so angry he's bound to make mistakes."

"Taking him along Thomas?"

"A driver!"

"She might be able to overdub with the God father theme tune."

"Not giving him a weapon then?"

"No certainly not, he might shoot his toes off."

"Yes, a you tube video, interview a bloke all in black narrating the good news, London is coming for you, or something like that."

"Wouldn't Jimmy get sore?" asked Winstanley.

"Ah, thank you Mr Winstanley, best not wake the animals in the zoo should we."

"Are they?"

"Oh yes sir, best leave the beasts to their prey."

He looked at Mr Black for an explanation of Billys mouth.

Mr Black smiled back at him, "A hundred miles an hour, I think he even talks in his sleep, cockney, they're all like this down here in London."

"Normal here abouts then?"

"Yep, but the kid has talents, and we can all drink at the well, right?"

BILLION'S 71

"Yes Thomas, so give me a date here?"

"Two days hence, New York City, you pick up the lads and supply, I'll show up later with rent a gob, my new driver, good for you?"

"Yes Thomas, so the money, is right?"

"Yes Mr Winstanley, that's the wife's department, natural in these things, I do the hunter gathering and she does the housework, sweet eh?"

"Ok, Thomas, see you in two days, and into the job, yes?"

"Yes John, don't be late!"

He turned and walked off with Billy at his side, Billy wanted to say something, but Mr Black pinched his arm to shut up until they were out of hearing distance.

"I get the feeling that you don't like him boss."

"I don't know him and so that's wise to distrust a stranger, don't you think young man, and why all the mouth?"

"Provocation, I just wanted to see what he's got boss, nothing more, the same as you, asking for the impossible, right?"

"So, you see that in me then Mr Grey?"

"I'm more valuable alive Mr Black, money and brain all mashed up."

Mr Black tried to kick him, but he ran off laughing.

"You will be mashed up you little shit, if you embarrass me like that again."

"It's just business Mr Black, we push and shove, all part of the game."

"So, who taught you the game?"

"East end brat, comes good and gets a trade, then gets lucky and marries a blond bombshell, who's very good with numbers, been ducking and diving all my working life Mr Black, some of it must have rubbed off somewhere don't you think?"

He stopped and waited for Mr Black to get close to him, "So why all the demands from the yank?"

Mr Black smiled, "Quick eh, kid, I feel things, and I listen to those feelings, safety feeling get it, so I pre plan for betrayal, just in case and hope it doesn't happen, so I'm not shocked by it all, get me?"

"One step ahead, just like the average rat then?" said Billy, before running off across the park before Mr Black caught him and beat the crap out of him.

He caught Billy in just a few strides by the neck, "At heart I'm just a teacher and I feel that you are going to be a star of the circus, but I also feel that if you survive, you might just make life hard for many of us."

"Only the bad and damned ugly Mr Black!" he ran off again, but while laughing, it all made Mr Black feel old in the presence of youth.

He ran after him again and caught him.

"Sorry Mr Black, these things come into my head and have to come out to be talked about, that's not wrong, is it?"

"No son, not wrong at all, keep the brain thinking at all times, so, an independent supply over there is not wrong, is it?"

"No boss, let him work for his bill, but he knew Jimmy down east, so presumably he knows Frank, right?"

"Yes, good lad, let's talk to Frank! A good stir up in the States would mean that all his troops would gather together, the more the merrier, and that's good if we want to annihilate them, right?"

"Yes, but a harder nut to crack, Mr Grey."

"I'm a man of machines, I'll come up with something Mr Black, the harder the shell the more brittle it is and easier to crush in one go."

"You boy are doing my head in, give the gob a rest and get into the bloody car!"

Mr Black drove them off and was enjoying the silence when Billy had another thought.

"So, this Don over there has the willies, partly by losing his money and part because he has other families on his back, so that would place us smack bang in the middle, a smart man could deal with them both and get them to destroy each other in the process, correct?"

Mr Black growled as him to shut up.

"So, Jimmy the saw could come in handy, all that money taken from under his nose, can't be good to claim you run London and this happens can it Mr Black?"

"So, he'll have feelers out searching for the culprits as well then?" said Mr Black.

"So, two more things we've learned this fine morning, this Don has the real hump, and Winstanley has to take sides for his own preservation back in the States, so it could be a double cross all the way along Mr Black, best be aware, ok?"

Mr Black growled again at him to shut up and give him some peace.

"And Jimmy is involved, regardless of what Frank says, we'll have to contact him when the times right, ok?"

"When?"

"When he's useful for our plan, bing, bang, bosh!"

CHAPTER 12 ... BRITISH AIRWAYS FLIGHT 7089 TO NEW YORK.

"I was in the scouts you know!" said Billy as the plane leveled off and he could see the ground at 30.000 feet below them.

"And do you know the moto?"

"Be prepared!" said Mr Black, then put his earphones on and pressed for the film to start on the screen in front of him.

"Correct, so, are we prepared?"

"All plans change in the face of the enemy kid, remember that one."

"So, what's the point of planning in the first place then?"

"Getting in the mood, finding resources, practicing first actions, and reactions to actions."

"Like a chess game?"

"Yes, ever played?"

"No, I never had the time and didn't see the point in the first place."

Mr Black took off the earphones, "Now that's classic lower class time management syndrome, I'm too busy earning to progress in your toffy nosed world."

"I don't get you?"

"It means, get off your arse and learn the trade."

"What trade?"

"War, because that's what we're about Mr Grey, war, so clear your mind, plan and scrub a plan, then plan some more just in case."

"Because of the war?"

"Yes, and the guilt of failure, now that's altogether another subject that you are not old enough to learn just yet."

"What if no mistakes are made?"

"Shut up, put your headphones on and watch this crappy film!"

Billy focused on the tittles rolling in front of him, "Titanic?"

"Just in case of failure boy!"

"And what's the point?"

"Watch the captain Mr Grey, he goes down with the ship, that's what officers do, failure to protect your people and you go down with the ship for incompetence, Captain Smith fully understood that point, get it?"

"And you Mr Black?"

"Death or glory Mr Grey, death or glory!"

Mr Black handed him card with the plan layout for New York City, "Driver Mr Grey, that's your job and they are your points and places of emergency pickups, clear?"

"Sir, yes sir!"

"And cut the American crap please, we are out of towners and that's our cover, clear?"

"Between you and me Mr Black, I think that our Frank wants to kill Jimmy the saw, past slight I would imagine, now how can we use that in some way?"

Mr Black turned up his volume and tried to ignore him.

"Yes, Mr Black, the timings will present themselves as we progress."

Mr Blacks hand squeezed Billy's knee to shut him up, so Billy took a nap and a calm thinking session, eventually he was slobbering down the side glass window, and Mr Black fell asleep watching a ship sinking and it reminded him of his life, so he slipped into the normal nightmare and swimming through the all too familiar pink lake of blood.

CHAPTER 13 ... STATELY HOME OF THE MARQUIS OF STAMFORD.

The downstairs parlor was set out for their business use, Sandra walked around and round as she thought about what Billy would be up to with all those animal who work for Mr Bloodworth.

A tailed waiter came in with a gold tray of tea and cakes, he placed them down on the table and looked to Gerald for further instructions, "Would that be all sirs?"

" Yes, thank you Anderson, so what time is lunch?"

"12.30 sir, and I thought a picnic in the grounds sir, down near the pond, good for you?"

Gerald looked at Sandra for the final decision, she gave him the face that would sour milk.

"Err, a splendid thought Aderson, but I think that it would be better in here, a bit busy you see."

"As you wish sir, we are on call as required sir." He walked out in silence, leaving Sandra to pour the tea for them.

"Women's work, that's how he thinks, you can be mummy, he's old school darling."

She ignored him knowing that he was just trying to entertain himself by winding her up.

She bent over and picked up the elegant sea serpent teapot and started to pour it into the highly decorated cups sitting on frilly saucers.

Gerald smiled at her, "Dresden, I'd say about 1780, totally irreplaceable by the way, so don't break any please Sandra darling."

She poured his tea and rattled the teacup with the spout just to wind him up, his panic was warming her mood a little.

But then she thought of Billy again, "So where the hell is he, and why hasn't he rung me by now?"

Mr Wilson ignored them both as he tapped away at his laptop, muttering and swearing under his breath.

"What's up with bollock brain, he seems unusually human today?"

"They won't let him into his desk this early to trade on the stocks, Wall street took a dive and lost points to the pound at the weekend, and he wants to get a bite on the dollar before they open."

"Moron!"

Her phone suddenly pinged at the side of her, she snatched it and scanned what was happening, she smiled at him, "A text, notification, Swiss bank, I just love them blokes, polite, smart, and very clean, I don't know why you don't like them, Geraldo?"

"Lack of remorse, or even a conscience perhaps?"

She looked at Wilson for an explanation of his remarks, he shrugged, "Oh don't ask or we'll get an hour of his moaning on and on about the Germans using Swiss banks to launder their stolen Jewish money during the second world war, I tend to agree with him though."

"The financial backbone of the new Europe!" said Gerald, "And Jewish gold and stolen monies, we deal with these scum bags over the years! So, when the Germans bit the dust, they said nothing, all lost in the system they say, not our money they say, we simply hold it for returning clients, when they fully know that their scumbag clients are dead, cold handshakes, give you the chills, and now the EU uses that to prop up their failing car plants and steel industries, we're the bloody clowns of Europe! We are the only ones who play by the rules, well they can all sod off because we're out of their Mafia led euro empire!"

"And Mrs. T?" said Wilson, he grinned over to Sandra as she watched Gerald in his meltdown.

"Yes, and the fishing rights that she fought so hard to regain, they still have the right to fish in the Yarmouth wash, we should have gone to war over that one!"

"Gangsters and morons, the lot of them, thieves by other names, no sense of humor, nothing, cold hearted you, see?"

"That's why we quit you know, what they really wanted in Brussels was the city of London stock exchange, the key to the world economy you see?"

He stopped chuntering and looked at them staring at him, "Sorry, just a blip, please excuse my mantras."

"Bonkers!" said Sandra, "So where the bloody hell is he?"

Gerald sat up and smiled, "If any of you lack wisdom, let him ask of God who will chastise not, but let him ask in faith, for he who lacks faith will be tossed as the sea even as a drunken man: James 1:5 and 6, James was the brother of Jesus you know, and his epistle should have come before Mathews, but he was ignored, Vatican politic, same old crap!"

She stared at him again as if he had lost the plot.

Wilson grinned, "Oh, he's onto his Bible quotes now, it's a sign of his nerves, Gerald, why don't you start the business projection planning for our city scraper, we need the bumf for the city planners, and you know how complicated it can get down the planning office?"

Gerald was now smiling at him, "Oh, yes, we need to drum up interest in living in a high-rise apartments overlooking the river Thames, yes, stroll down to your favorite restaurant, see the lights and the views of our great city from on high! The show town and the opera, the 24/7 lifestyle of the modern 21st century man!"

"Will you shut up!" shouted Sandra, you are getting on my tits!"

Her phone pinged again, she snatched it up and read the text out loud.

"Armageddon one is rolling across the pond, I'm in the planning, make ready the payment runs, ready for the conclusion of the contract or I'm a dead man, best not disappoint the staff, love Billy."

She wiped her sweaty hands on the white tablecloth and stared at the two men.

"Ok, stop what you're doing and prep for the payments run."

"And who made you the big cheese around here?" said Gerald.

"You lot when you planned to steal too much bloody money, literally, bloody money!"

Mr Wilson smiled at her, "Panic not madam, we have plenty to splash around, the more the merrier and all that?"

"And what the hell does that mean?"

"The tax man Sandra!" said Gerald, "We have to avoid the dreaded at all costs."

"What?" she squeaked.

"We seek em here we seek em there; we seek them everywhere!"

"What's he on?"

"I offer my best new brand of confusion for the guppy with all the dosh in the world."

"He's bonkers!"

"No dear," said Wilson, "He has a system that will confuse and caused panic in the markets, and as we all know, to get them to panic gets us to make money, and the cloud of dust will cover everything in the end."

"Money makes the world go round, world go round, world go round!" Gerald was now singing his favorite song.

"But what if he gets killed darling, do we still pay or what?"

She stared at them in sudden horror and panic, "Then I will kill you, and you!"

"But after I've done the transfers though?"

"Well yes, but I'm still going to kill you and you!"

"But the money darling, it has to breathe and earn and bring wealth to millions, we have responsibilities all over darling."

"He had better not be in the middle of all this or I will kill him myself!"

"Panic not, that woman, Mr Bloodworth will be doing all the slaughtering."

It stopped her and made her think, she stared Gerald down and cooled down herself, "This is not right is it, Geraldo?"

"We stood on the dragons tail darling; we can do nothing else but defend the mother lode."

"I might just kill you now Geraldo!" she stood up and chased him around before trying to throttle him on the sofa, her hands squeezed his neck as he gurgled, "But what about the transfers?" he choked.

"Best not kill the golden goose Sandra," said Wilson, "Hey, I'm in, thank you US treasury, I love you really!"

Sandra had to stop trying to kill Gerald and laugh, he screeched in laughter with her.

"Panic not sweetheart, he's a clever boy and clever boys make better bankers!" said Wilson now concentrating on his investments, "Oh damn and blast, the Dollar has revived!"

"You lot are all bonkers!" screeched Sandra.

CHAPTER 14 ... JFK AIRPORT NEW YORK ... USA.

Winstanley watched and waited as the crowds of men shuffling through the customs hall and the final plastic curtain to the exit lounge, the press were there taking photos of the stars as they mingled with ordinary folk and strutted with their friends.

He held up a sign that read (English five a side league) he counted them off as the gathered, then pointed to the minibus through the giant glass windows.

He recounted the ten heads as they climbed aboard the minibus, he had received instructions not to speak to them and not to entertain them in any way, no food and no drink, their instructions would follow.

He jumped into the driver's seat and drove off to the freeway, then pressed for the tv screen to roll down and start to play.

Mr Bloodworth's face started the giggling, but as if he were there, they stopped when he became serious and focused on them with the white bushy eyebrows of seriousness.

"Welcome, brethren to the big apple, because we are about to take a bite, so listen up."

"Mr Driver has supplied the gear needed for the job, and it's under your seats, weapons and ammunition, so saddle up and be ready for the first contact."

Mr Driver will drop you all off at the bus station, to be reunited in five days, Mr Brown commands, all decisions go through him, we have a new member, a Mr Grey and he is part of the planning committee and will be along shortly after the New York engagement."

"The job starts in five days in Miami, all will be ready to go, Mr Grey will instruct on new equipment needed for this complicated work, Mr Orange, maps and routes please, Mr green, security as usual, including the new base of operations, and a good cover story is needed for a group of Brits to be there, clear?"

"In your cases are instructions for Miami, a good amount of cash for you to buy a vehicle perhaps, I leave all that to you, contact rules apply, no women, no drink, no trouble, any infringement of contact rules and I will.......?"

"Beat the crap out of that color!" echoed the van load of men in unison.

"Behave on site as gentlemen because I believe under all that bullshit, I've taught you, you could well be gentlemen."

"Miami is the new base of operations."

"And yes, I realize that work done, and all that study for New York, just homework and it might be needed in the future, so nothing lost in your study time."

"A slight change of the plan, so I need two volunteers for a little engagement in the city, that's Mr Red and Mr Blue, I knew you would be the first to volunteer, and use the new body armor, the army tell me it's very good, Mr Driver will explain the details."

"Ok, good luck everyone, so to be on time one has to be ....?"

"Early!" shouted the passengers in unison.

"We are not friends, we are not buddies, we are ....?"

"Brethren!" echoed the bus.

"I don't even like you, because you are ....?"

"Scum of the earth!" echoed down the bus.

"So, in two's as always, I protect his back as ....?

"He protects mine!" shouted the passengers, then started laughing as the screen blacked out.

Winstanley listened to the conversation and the mantra replies, he was impressed with the English discipline and silently watched them in the driver's mirror, after the mumbling and laughing they got down to arming themselves with the equipment supplied.

"My name is Mr Driver, so we are ten away from the bus station, but he has left cash for you to buy cars if needed, personally I would buy a truck, but that's me, but I advise not to roll up to one dealer as a mob and buy all his 4/4 stock, a bit too obvious, I leave that to you guys."

"Mr Red and Mr Blue are with me to go into the city on another matter, and a pre curser for the main action, again gentlemen, good luck and do not be too obvious, my advice is to speak very few words to the natives, your various British accents could send alarm waves through the city if they hear you, ok guy, be ready to dismount!"

He stopped the bus and counted them off one by one and watched them disperse in different directions, they just disappear in front of his eyes into the public domain.

Both Mr Red and Mr Blue watched him close up as he watched their Brethren depart.

"Not worked with us before then Mr Driver?" asked Mr Red.

He smiled at him before answering, "And you want me to answer that?"

Mr Red laughed, "Yeah, sorry!"

"So where to then?" asked Mr Blue.

"Back to JFK to pick up the big guy and his new best buddy."

Mr Red winked at Mr Blue to shut him up before he asked the obvious question.

CHAPTER 15 ... THE MAYFAIR CLUB ... LONDON.

The interior and the music of the Mayfair club overpowered conversation as the three of them walked on, through the music sound stage to a corridor at the back, Frank handed out the ear buds for Ned and Max to place in their ears, "Plug in and pretend you are connected to the outside world, do not poke or touch it too often because that tells them that you are new to this game."

Folow my lead in and around the club, you do not see anything in this place, you do not smoke or laugh or even talk, swagger, you are the boys, you own the place, give it the cockney strut, got me boys?"

They both nodded in nervousness, and he waited for the smile of confidence from each of them.

Ned put his hand up to ask something and Frank smiled to hear him.

"Err .... why are we doing this again?"

"Well because we have very important information the Jimmy the saw!"

"So, dose he?"

"What saw people up into little sections to be thrown into the Thame, the answer is yes, regularly, any other stupid questions lads?"

They nervously followed him into the heart of clubland through various doorways until they came to a steel bolted heavy door, painted red, with the number one in gold letters on top of the spy hole.

"Ok, listen up, not one single word comes out of your mouths, no matter what, or I'll look an idiot having a night out with my gay friends, do not sit, do not take your eyes off Jimmy, just one ho ha or fart from you, and I will punch you in the mush on the spot, got that?"

"This is full on business, get me boys?"

They nodded in silence before he knocked on the door, they waited in silence, he knocked again.

The door squeaked open, and a giant stared down at them from the light within, "What?" said the man in the doorway causing the shadow over them.

"You are bloody useless as an assistant Shrek, brains of a can of beans!" said Frank.

"And?" said the man as he stared at them.

"Frank, just a home visit to my grandad Jimmy the chain saw, personal, get me Shrek?"

"You and the girls can fuck off!"

Frank stepped back and showed the monster his best boys.

"Ok lads, teach Moby Dick a lesson on management consultancy!"

A shout came from the office inside, "Oh for fucks sake Danny, you are supposed to let people in to ask questions and all that, and not tell them to fuck off, this is work, you stupid slug!"

Big Danny moved out of the way and Frank and his crew walked in to see and man sitting at his desk smoking a cigar, he didn't get up, but just sat there staring at them.

"What is it, the circus in town or are you struggling for staff Jim?"

Recognition was now in Jimmies yes, "Franky fingers, come to pay respects to your grandpa, eh?"

"I thought I might see the old place again Jim, nothing's changed, has it?"

Jim smiled at him and understood that the game was on.

"Franky boy, I was told that after your last stint at Her Majesty's displeasure you went east and changed addresses, forgot your old mate then, why was that?"

"Na, just sick of the scintillating convos down here in the cellar, I had to find dry land and stand up normal like and walk on two feet like we're supposed to do, right?"

"You've turned sour Frank, what is it, not making any money in the car game?"

"No, I just didn't want to live like Dracula anymore, I found the heat and light of the sun to be good for me."

"Sour Frank, no need to be rude boy!"

"Hey, it's an emergency visit, to import information Jim, that's it, I must owe you a favor somewhere down the line, right?"

"Yes, you bloody do Frank, and no respect that I can remember, so what is it you have to whisper?"

"Out of old-time respect Jim, I just pass on the bad news from a friend."

"Your friend or mine?"

"Both Frank, did you hear about the English bloke stabbed in the back by a Yank, friends supposedly, but they were not Jim, they wanted his Kingdom, something about security for their washing machine, get me?"

"And that's news boy?"

"They are recruiting Frank, big lads, useful lads, and paying in American, big bucks, get me?"

"Who?"

"Well, no friends of mine Jim, perhaps they're yours?"

"And this is your statement of what?"

"Big smoke in the city Jim, big problems for those damn Yanks losing a great big lump apparently, bloody obvious really, I would have thought, anyway, job done, that's me Jim, if you want the Roller washed and valeted just give me a call mate, ok?"

"How much?"

"Well, he just has to ask his friends don't he Jim, none of mine and all that."

"Big threats?"

"Well, the top dog in NYC, I'm told, too much money I think Jim, it sends em bonkers don't it mate!"

"I'll make a call then?"

"Best check it out mate, after all what would happen to this place if Big Jim was downed?" he thumbed to Big Danny, "A new management consultancy group obviously, right?"

"Thank for your concern Frank, so do I owe you anything for this?"

"Now that would be rude to ask, don't you think Jim, a favor asked is a gift given, yes?"

Jim stared at him as he stubbed out his cigar, "Any names handy?"

"American accents Jim, Italian types, not good I think, the Turks could be coming south maybe? I don't know thankfully."

Jim smiled at him, "The Hulk will see you out Frank, you really surprise me boy with all this shit you bring to my door, you have really changed son with all this shit stirring, you didn't used to be like this."

"Hey Jim, I could have stayed silent and be an enemy of my old friend, but I thought no, that's not good to let friends down like that, so I'm here, did I do wrong Jim?"

"No Frank and I'll pay a visit if you don't mind, a service did you say?"

"And a complete valet for my oldest friend Jim, a little smiley air freshener and all!"

Jim flicked his finger to the door for Danny to escort him and his boys out.

The door slammed behind them, and they walked off back into the maze of corridors again.

"Well, that's the spanner thrown into the gearbox, so let's see how it settles here in the city." said Frank.

"You don't like him do you Frank?" asked Max.

"Frank turned to him, "No one likes a monster, but we all have to live with one to survive, right?"

"Err ... yes boss, understood, but he'll check it all out with others though?"

"Of course he will, that's the point, our Billy wants them to distrust each other, part of the greater plan I think."

"And you trust Billy?"

"With my life son, and so should you."

"Is he really that dangerous?"

"Shut it you moron!"

The lads had listened to the conversation and looked at each other as they exited the building to be able to breathe the smelly London air and feel better about living.

Frank put his arms around their necks, "Right lads, back to the garage, now have any of you ever change the oil and filter on a Jaguar before?"

"But Lord whatsits place?"

"Oh, come on lads, too boring for me anyway, come, let's get a drink, while were in town, I'm buying."

"But Mr Blood insisted Frank!" said Max.

"Hey, this is London and it's my town, so shut up and get it down your neck!"

CHAPTER 16 ... MANHATTEN NEW YORK CITY ... USA.

Mr Driver stopped the minibus and smiled at Mr Grey, "In America we drive on the wrong side of the road as you can see, ok with that?"

Billy was about to give him a mouthful of abuse, but the noise came from the back seats as Mr Black tried to get into his body armour, "What the hell's wrong with you Driver, I've got Danny DeVito's bloody short-arsed armour, oh bollocks to it all," he ripped it off and threw it into the corner in disgust.

Billy had to laugh, but the stare from the big man shut him up, instantly.

"Anyway!" said Mr Black, "Why would I need body armour, it's the uglies in there who need that, let's get to the killing, I'm getting bored her with you lot!"

Mr Blue and Mr Red giggled at the old man's frustration but said nothing, they had learned the hard way to be silent when he was in a rage before a job.

"So how are we breaking into this flat then?" said Billy.

"What's this we business? There is no we here, you are the new driver, so take the wheel and shut the fuck up!"

Billy noticed the colour men in the back look away instead of listening to his bollockings by Mr Black, he knew that they would be laughing at him but seemed silent.

"You, pick us up as directed Mr Grey and keep the opinions to yourself!"

Mr Black defied him to make any comment with the full-on stare.

"Ok, Mr Grey, you, go around the block, slowly and return to this spot three times, give us time to do our work, be ready for a quick pick up, we should have a lot of things to burn up there so don't panic if you see smoke, clear?"

"Clear boss!"

"And if the place seems to be in meltdown, then wait for us in position two down by the river, clear?"

"Yes boss!"

Mr Black gave him the eyes to make sure he did what he was told to do, "No risks, no bad parking, no wheel's spinning, be the grey man you are, yes?"

"Yes boss! I'm on the coms if there's a problem down here, yes?"

"Such as what Mr Grey?"

"Well re-enforcements perhaps, or the cops surround the place, just anything like that."

"Just do as you're told Mr Grey, that is enough for now!" he looked around at his team.

"Ready to execute plan A gentlemen?"

All three of them nodded, "Ok, let's roll......go!"

He stepped out and quickly walked away to the office block buttoning up his long raincoat as he went, the others followed close behind.

Billy jumped into the vacant driver's seat and watched them go into the building; their long coats flapped in the sudden breeze.

"Good luck Mr Black," he mumbled as he watched the other traffic coming and going in the night.

CHAPTER 17 ... MANHATTAN HEIGHTS ... NEW YORK CITY.

They chose the lift to go to the top floor, but another man tried to get in with them, Mr Black grabbed the man's shirt collar and threw him out, the colour men laughed at the shocked lift traveller, but Mr Black turned and gave them the face.

The man stood and watched in shocked silence as the doors closed and the lift ascended.

The lift doors opened on the 30th floor and a big man tried to stop Mr Black from coming onto that floor, he said something but didn't get a chance to speak as a knife was thrust up through the man's lower jaw and into his mouth pallet driving it up with shear power.

"On your toes big lad, or this could go into your brain cavity in a second, now today's simple question is this, where does he live and is he home?"

The man tried to struggle through the excruciating pain and tried to speak, "No!"

"To both eh, and camera protected?"

The man tried to nod through the pain, but a small automatic put him out of his misery as Mr Black pulled the trigger with his other hand, the man dropped to the floor dead.

He nodded to Mr Red to knock on the door, "Well you never know lads, sometime, maybe?"

Mr Red knocked and stood back as machine gun bullets blasted through from the inside of the building.

Mr Blue put the charge on the door lock and stood to the other side of the door as it blasted into the room.

Mr Blue was now on the floor and firing into the room killing the occupants before Driver and Mr Black stepped over him and walked in firing, the room was now full of the dead, and the fumes

"I was expecting more action here Mr Driver, so where is Mr Vigo?"

Mr Driver shrugged, "He's a fool if he's set us up here Mr Black, I'll kill the little bastard."

"Let's be calm, he might have his family as hostage, we never know do we?"

"God damn it, all he had to do was keep his mouth shut, that's it!"

"These Mafiosi might be smarter that we think Mr Driver and they have leverages on some of our informers, so we are given away, all is not lost however, so to the grand bonfire gentlemen, get on with it please!"

Mr Red and Mr Blue rifled through the office paperwork trying to find something of value to their cause, "Nothing boss!"

"Ok, burn it, the lot!" he pushed over a large bookcase and threw a couple of bottles of whiskey into the books, they smashed and soaked in.

"Anyone have a light, none of us smoke anymore, really strange, eh?"

Mr Driver laughed at him then found the cigar lighter on the desk and started the fire going, Mr Blue had found the drinks cabinet and threw the bottles onto the plush carpet as the fire took hold.

The flames quickly taking hold of the antique furniture as he turned over the desk and all the papers into the flames.

"Ok, out and be gone, same route out please!"

As they got back to the lift his phone pinged, "Yes Mr Grey?"

"An army is gathering out here boss, shotguns and small arms, heading your way, maybe thirty of them, should I divert to place B for pickup?"

"Yes Mr Grey, do that now and thank you for the heads up!"

"We've been betrayed lads, so down the corridor and the fire exit quick!"

They ran down the extended corridor to find the fire door bricked up.

"That shouldn't be there Mr Driver, should it?"

"Sorry, not on the plans, anywhere!"

"Yes, ok, we go down the stairs and abseil from one of the lower floors, did you bring insurances?"

Mr Driver grinned and opened his kit bag to reveal claymore mines and rope.

"Good lad, now set the dead man with a mine and send it down, yes?"

"As a present, yes, I like it Mr Black, now that's downright nasty man!"

Mr Black gave him the look to shut up and get on with it," And set a couple in the corridor for followers, yes?"

"Sir, yes, sir!"

Mr Driver set the mine to pull when the doors opened again on the ground floor then pressed the button to send it down, they were waiting for him then they all ran off down the stairs.

On the 4th floor they could hear the shouting and screaming coming from the ground floor.

"Ok, Mr Blue, set the rope for the climb down please."

Mr Blue tied the rope to the radiator bracket on the wall and gave it a tug to check if it were good, then nodded to them.

"Ok, out and reassemble in the car park."

He was the last to descend to the floor near the garbage bins, "Mr Driver was ready to run for the bus, but Mr Red grabbed his arm, and nodded to Mr Black, "Annihilation sir, remember?"

As Mr Blacks feet touched down, he was reloading his weapon then looked at them to check if they had done the same, "Ready?"

Heads nodded and followed him firing from the hip as they mowed down the men holding guns and waiting to ambush the people doing the shooting.

They ran over the dead bodies and waited for Mr Driver to throw his mines into the lobby and kill some more people, those still standing were killed by Mr Black at the back of them.

He emptied a full clip into all the glass and furniture just in case of people hiding from the shooting.

"Ok gents, pickup point B please, and withing the hour, problems then leave it to point C in four hours, clear everyone?"

He let the MP5 swing on its shoulder strap back under his arm, he felt the heat of the gun barrel on his arm as he buttoned up his coat and walked off into the darkness of the night, calmly walking a fast pace away from the site of destruction, each one going in a different direction doing the same and stepping into shadows as cars flashed by.

Walking away they could all see the flames take hold of the top floor and the black smoke billowed into the city streets clogging the place up with acrid smoke.

The sounds of the city now changed to whoops of fire engines and police cars blasting through the streets here and there during the potential rescue of people trapped up top.

None were eventually found alive amongst the glass and bloody fragments of dead men and cold guns.

Mr Black heard a couple of pops he thought might be gunfire but thought nothing of it as he got to the river and Billy smoking a cigar leaning on a wall waiting for them.

He crept up to him and tore the burning cigar from his mouth and threw it into the river.

"DNA evidence and very stupid to take up smoking, what would Sandra say if you came home and had that habit again, wrong on all points numb-nuts!"

"Get in the bastard bus and get the engine warmed up!"

CHAPTER 18 ... FOOT FERRY ... PIER 3 ... HUDSON RIVER CROSSING.

Billy dutifully started the bus engine up and sat there with Mr Black for the others to return, he looked at his watch from time to time and could tell that Mr Black was getting madder and madder with the waiting.

"I heard pops, did you hear pops? asked Mr Black.

"In the distance, I thought it was you lot, cornered by cops or something."

"Can you drive fast son?"

"I'm a mechanic, and all mechanics can drive fast, it's how we test the kit, vroom, vroom and all that."

Mr Black was listening to the sounds of the city as he waited, "I don't like this, not good, not professional at all."

"Five to time out boss!" said Billy.

"Shit, where the hell are they? If they've got lost, I will bloody kill them!"

"That's it boss, times up, we need to roll sir!"

"What's that?" he thumbed to a distant footfall, then suddenly Mr Driver was at the door and dived in and sat down, "Cops, caught us on the road, the guys got caught in crossfire, sorry Thomas!"

Mr Black stared at him then nodded for Billy to get going, "Be gone Billy!"

Billy drove off into the dark night on the riverbank road, but his brain was working at a hundred miles an hour, Mr Black had just broken name protocol and so had Mr Driver, he was alarmed at the changes and knew something was going to happen and soon.

"So how did it go?" asked Mr Black.

"Well, we all seemed to collide in a sweet spot the cops had covered, and they started firing at us, no cover, we were dead men running, I just escaped, the guys took head shot, sorry guy, they're dead man!"

"And the body armour?"

Well as I just said, head shots man, no chance."

Mr Black turned to Billy, "Ok, Mr Grey, take us to action scene two please."

Mr Driver looked alarmed suddenly, "But we're early for that one, we planned for an 08.00 entry, remember Mr Black?"

"Yes, but I've just changed the plan to hit them early before the bad news hits the morning headlines and the rats go down their holes, we get them while we're fresh, understood?"

"Long distance shots?"

"What?"

"Did the cops use long distance shot to the heads?"

"Err yeah, I suppose, I was just trying to get away man!"

"Lucky shots?"

"No, they seemed like they'd set an ambush, Vigo again you think?"

"And he knows our plans Mr Driver?"

"Well, no, stupid idea!"

Mr Black watched Mr Drivers every eye movement and watched him as he reloaded his small arms Heckler and Coch."

"They have suppressors on them in the army you know?"

"Do they Mr Black, for why?"

"Close action, killing guards or something, but to get closer, you have to be very good with one of those don't you?"

Mr Driver was getting nervous with the questioning and the banter coming from Mr Black, so he suddenly loaded a slug in the chamber and was about to point it at Mr Black, but the blade appeared out of Mr Blacks sleeve and the dagger stuck into the neck and roof of Mr Drivers mouth as Mr Black held it there.

"An interesting feeling don't you think John?"

"Mr Driver was incapacitated with so much agony he couldn't answer."

"So, you killed my boys, part of a greater plan?"

Billy watched him in the mirror in horror as Mr Driver grunted in excruciating agony, the knife now through both pallets and partly into his brain cavity, Mr Drivers eye flickered like his lights were going out.

"Oh, I know, you organised a double bubble payout from another Mafia Don, you sold our boys out and us as well, a sweetener, eh?"

Mr Driver tried to say something, but Mr Black pushed the knife into his brain and twisted it around, the man was now dead, but his body wriggled in death throws, still wanting to live without its brain.

Billy watched in silent mind melting horror as he killed the man then started stripping him naked.

"Ok, turn around Billy and go back to site B please, we have to throw out the trash!"

Billy turned round the vehicle in one go on the wide road and headed back to the river.

"Is that how my turn comes Mr Bloodworth, stabbed when the payout is ended and you're filthy rich?"

Mr Black pointed the knife at him, "Now stop that Billy, he sold us out, and wanted to get paid twice, understood, he had another contract and we were the sweetener for the deal, possibly Franks mate down the east end, so cut the blab and get us back there, the lads are possibly only wounded and waiting for his other contractors to come and finish the job on them, clear?"

"Yes boss, very clear! Sorry for asking that?"

"It's ok boy, death can be shocking, this scumbag very nearly got us all in a sack, clever don't you think, getting paid two times for the same job?"

"Yes, but he killed all those other blokes, right?"

"Yes true, but they were from another family over west perhaps and another big wig with plenty of money."

Billy pulled up and stopped the bus as he saw scene of death close up and personal.

"But he wouldn't have gotten mine boss?"

Mr Black stared him down after finishing stripping the dead man, "Really, and you think that rubbish, really?"

Billy stared back at him, "Sandra, right?"

"Oh, yes and the rest of your family and friends, one at a time, this is the reality of this work, sorry to be so blunt at a time like this, but just look at this, the reality and failure for yourself, this could be us or any of us, you me, or the colours, this is our work, get used to it or get out of it, that was once said to be in the very same situation and I had to decide for myself, so now, it's your turn, so what'll it be, Billy Boncour?"

He nodded to the dead man, as Billy looked on horrified.

Mr Black gave him a couple of breaths before he raised his voice again, "Ok, move it back to the river, now!"

Billy knocked it in gear again and pulled off at speed, leaving Mr Black to mop up the blood with the dead man's clothes.

He watched him in the mirror in shock at his complete callous behaviour, having just killed the man only seconds before.

Mr Black stared up at him again, "Come on, move it, get us there and fast."

CHAPTER 19 ... THE HUDSON RIVER ... PIER 3 ... FOOT CROSSING.

Billy parked the bus in the same spot, Mr Black pointed for him to get closer to the river and waved him back from the back seats before coming forward and throwing the body into the dark flow of the Hudson river, he watched the corpse float away, he had always thought that a dead body would sink but it didn't and watched as Mr Black slammed the door and looked at him.

He then ran off, Billy was now fully panicked and didn't know what to do if Mr Black didn't return, he thought about the time he was thrown into the Canary wharf in London, for fun, by so called friends who were older and so called wiser and he realised that he was a kid in the wrong gang, so he quit that gang and joined another where they were his age, but they were a bunch of drips so he went alone.

Thinking about this experience made him think of Sandra, oh, she was a bully in all but name, her way or the motorway, was one of her lines, but he loved that about her, and she was fiercely loyal to the family and him, and he knew it was to the death with her, he loved her for that as well.

He also knew that if he betrayed her, then he would be floating down a river somewhere.

He smiled to himself as he thought about his new life with these monsters, "Am I in the wrong gang again?" he mumbled to himself, but the noise of the door being opened again stopped all thoughts, Mr Black suddenly opened the sliding door and pulled in the two-colour men and grunted to get going.

"Mr Red had been shot in the neck and was bleeding all over the place and Mr Blue had a thigh wound and was groaning in pain.

"Move it, Billy!" shouted Mr Black. Now wanting action and fast.

He put it in gear and put his foot down, racing through town.

"Slow down and find a lamp post to shine lights on me and the lads, I have to operate on them."

"Yes boss," Billy was now up to speed as he looked an eventually found a giant shopping centre with lights just stating up for early shoppers.

"Ok, stop and hold till I've done this!"

He watched Mr Black operate on the men, first by pulling out the slug in Mr Red's neck and shoulder area, he was fascinated how good Mr Black was, when done he filled the hole with gauze and simply put a plaster over it.

"Don't you need to stitch that sir?"

He received the black stare from the old man as Mr Red laughed at his innocence.

Mr Blue then grunted as Mr Black put another probe into the gunshot wound and tried to find the bullet, he bit onto the seat belt to somehow relieve the pain, but trying to take away some of the shock of being operated on and grinning in agony as Mr Black probed the wound, he asked, "So where's Driver?"

"In the river Mr Blue, he roused the unforgiving nature of Mr Black and now he sleeps with the fishes!"

"What?"

"He's the one who shot you boy!" said Mr Black, "That bastard was on a double bubble!"

Mr Blue looked to Billy for an explanation.

"He was playing us, "said Billy "Very clever really except he bumped into one who is even more nasty in Mr Black, who takes thing very bad with being betrayed."

He looked to Mr Black to get a clearer description of the details, but Mr Black was concentrating on finding the slug and making a mess of his upper thigh as Mr Blue agonised in the pain.

"He was working for another Don with secret ambitions to run the city, by having us kill him and take the credit, smart, eh? Greed kills you see, come to think of it, we could do that!"

Mr Black stopped what he was doing and looked at him, "And what is that?"

"Well, we visit site B and instead of terminating them we offer them a deal, from the other Don, see what I mean?"

Mr Red was now giggling at Billy, then they were all laughing.

"Do I shoot him or work for him lads?" said Mr Black.

He was now bandaging up Mr Blue and gave him some pills to take and a bottle of water to finish off in one go.

"Ok, Mr Grey, take me through that one again please? He asked.

"Ok, this Don whoever he is has a plan, obviously, and now he's going to see his boy floating down the river on the morning news, so what does he do, he runs down his rat hole in fear, because he's now thinking that we've sussed his little game, and we have, right?"

Mr Black stared at him in silence, "Ok, all very interesting, hotel, go now, go!"

Billy pulled off and headed uptown to their hotel on the other side of the city in the Bronx. "Yes, boss so why don't we be the middlemen and be as Frank suggested, we be the king makers?"

Mr Red started off the laughing again as they joined in, "Somebody shoot the bugger while we still can!" said Mr Black and the laughter increased.

"Mr Grey, shut up!"

"Ok, I've got it, so Mr Black can be bad cop and I'll be Mr Nice, all smiles and the deal maker, yes?"

"With whom?"

"The bankers, yes?"

"Mr Grey, shut the fuck up!"

He continued to drive them through the city and in minuets they were all asleep in the back, flaked out on the seats and the floor.

"So, I need a posh aftershave, none of that cheap crap, and I need Drivers rings as proof of his decline and his river trip!"

He looked in the mirror again and Mr Black had stuffed bandages in his ears to shut out the noise.

He pulled up at the motel and stopped the engine then looked in the mirror and buffed his teeth with the window rag, then checked again in the mirror, he thought of calling Mr Black Igor as an introduction to be the animal on site, but perhaps that would get him killed so he changed that plan and woke them up to move and get some rest.

They were all asleep in seconds, but his brain was running at a hundred miles an hour as he planned to change hearts and mind, so he went for a shower and tried to smarten himself up the for the mornings important meeting, he had it down before he came back and sat on his bed.

"What I need is a really posh suit, any ideas?"

"Shut...... the fuck ...... up!" screeched everyone.

In the early morning light Mr Black sat on the lounger soaking up the rising sun on the outside patio, his feet were in the hot tub, and he partly snoozed when he could.

"Ok, take me through this one more time."

Billy smiled that his plan was being considered.

"Ok, I'm good boy and you're the animal only just in control of killing everyone, angry you see from your betrayal, and these are the people who caused it all, get me?"

"Anyway, where does this banker bloke live?"

"Who?"

"This Vigo bloke, he has a family, right?"

"Err ... yeah, so what?"

"So anyway, when we enter, I do all the talking right?"

Mr Black couldn't keep his eyes open anymore and dozed off as Billy rumbled on and on and on.

Billy picked up the phone and rang the UK, and the garage to check on Frank.

Frank picked up, "Warren cars!"

"I knew you couldn't keep away!" said Billy.

"Well how long can you stand listening to banker jabbering on about tax incentives?"

"Yeah, agreed, so are you working?"

"Yes, JoJo's doing all the work, and he has two new niffys."

"Who?"

"Those banker wankers, who stole all the money and gave it to you, who would have thought that those two would take to servicing motors, I put em on a bonus for speed, they love it, they're now talking of expanding my business, they have brains kid, you just never know do you?"

"I've been thinking Frank, about you and your relationship with Jimmy the saw, bad, is it?"

"Well yes, it is now, after I passed on your latest little news, I hear he's looking for the Americans doing the recruiting on his turf, bodies down the river boy, stupid really taking the piss like that, anyway what was the thought of the day?"

"Well, another visit Frank, can you do that for me?"

"Oh, do me a favour Billy?"

"Look, just to pass on his new nickname, a friend would do that for him wouldn't he?"

"Oh, here we go, now what's he called?"

"Well shiny arse, well, he sits as Rome burns around his patch, and all that money taken under his nose like that, an no respect given or received, right?"

"Oh, get to the point of this Billy!"

"Look the Yanks stole 50 mill, from under his nose, not nice, and his so-called friends as well, not even a drink for his friendship Frank, how can he put up with that?"

"Ok, just give me the line here Billy, what is it you really want from the animal?"

"I want him over here Frank, I want him in the mix."

"Are you bonkers, you want Jimmy the saw on that side of the pond, what the hell for?"

"Well to get his money back, a company called ....err." he looked at his notes to read the company name. "Err .... Pierce and Vigo, here in New York, err ... corporate lawyers for the mob over here and they've taken Jimmy's share and that's 50 great big ones, get it?"

"And how did I find out all this Billy?"

"From me, on holiday mate, nice food by the way, burgers all the time, yumsville, anyway I bumped into an old pal, and he tells me that this Bobby Vigo is spending big, a new house, boat, cars for all his family, well it gets noticed right?"

"From what snatch?"

"Ours Frank, the one your new boys stole, his share was 50 mill, didn't I say?"

Frank held the phone in his ear for a second or two before speaking again, "No you bloody didn't say Billy, what the hell's happening over there?"

"A bit of a hitch, Mr Bloodworth's associate who was supposed to be helping us, betrayed us to other Mafia people, I'll sort that out later, but the point is this, Mr Winstanley now sleeps with the fishes, clear?"

"You'll sort it out? Sort what bloody out?" Frank screamed down the phone.

"Not to worry Frank, but the point is this, in about an hour or so the news will hit the headlines over here and there, man stabbed and stripped floating in the Hudson river, clear?"

"No, I'm not bloody clear?"

Suddenly the phone was snatched from Billy's ear and Mr Black spoke down the line to Frank, "Ok, listen up Frank, I had to throw out the trash into the river and Billy has gone bonkers, but good bonkers because we were in the shit and he has a plan to get us out of it, clear?"

"Not really Tom!"

"Just do it Frank, the kids a natural talent, so just do what he says, go and wind Jimmy up, we want him over here for some reason not yet explained to me, but anyway, just do it please!"

He handed the phone back to Billy, "Frank, does he still have sick note working for him?"

"Yes, and the normal animals he's keeps in a cage!"

"Ok, we need his full crew over here, they are taking the piss Frank, 50, from under his snout, do me a favour shiny arse, get me?"

"And what if he comes over there and starts killing people?"

Billy held the phone to let Frank think it through.

"He's not coming back is he Billy boy?"

"You are not the only one with a grudge Frank, anyway, call me on this line from now on, and do get him moving please!"

"Put him on Billy."

Billy handed over the phone again and Mr Black listened, "And you will ensure he does not use his return ticket?"

"Yes Frank, my responsibility, get it."

"And what about the vacuum he leaves?"

"Yours Frank, go into the city and take it, you know how it goes, and Billy will give you the credit for his loss to humanity."

"Put him on again Tom!"

He passed the phone back to Billy, "Are you stark raving bonkers sonny?"

"Look Frank, these people can do this, I'm one of the planners and I plan for his shallow grave, clear?"

"But for why boy?"

"Smoke and mirrors Frank and a cloud of dirty dust he will create as he enters the States, understood?"

"Not really son, but I'll have a chat with Jim and put him in the picture, quite a lump to lose, isn't it?"

"Embarrassing Frank, he's old school and due, agreed?"

Frank thought about it before answering him again, "And who will I owe for all this?"

"The colours Frank, Mr Bloodworth and his boys."

"And you Billy bonkers?"

"Just friendship Frank, you and me mate, yes?"

"Yes Billy, do it!"

"Switch the telly on Frank and check out the American news channels.

The phone was now dead in Billy's hand he turned to the face of Mr Black, "Yes Mr Black a good thought and Frank is perfect for all that, provided we clear the path, and we can, right?"

Mr Black nodded to him and Billy understood the grudge both he and Frank had for the man.

"None of my business, eh?"

"Correct squirt, now who is sick note?"

"Ah, the animal in the cage."

"What?"

"He's one of Jimmy's boy, psycho's the lot of them, but Sick note is the worst."

"And?" grunted Mr Black.

"Well, he's a Millwall fan, bonkers the lot of them, anyway, he's watching the game and next doors are having a garden party and he bangs on the wall to shut them up so he can hear the game, anyway someone must have told him the sod off or something and he was raging, then his team went down five nil, I mean football, a mugs game right?"

"And?" asked Mr Black.

"Well, he goes round to the neighbour's and kills them all, chops them up int little pieces, dog and all!"

"How many?"

"The whole family, three kids, him and his wife doing the barbi in the back yard, kills them all, so anyway, when he's arrested, he says to the cops that he hadn't had his medication and he's very sorry for the mess he's caused, then shows them his......."

"Sick note!" said Mr Black.

"Yep, so he gets detained on Her Majesties pleasure for life, unfit to plea in fact and he's Dartmoor bound, life without parole."

"Then a couple of years later, Jimmy rolls up in his camper van and collect's our sick note while he's out on a social working party in the forest, bing bang bosh, he's in the frame, central London, Jimmy even has the axe on his wall in the snug, he calls it his quiet time."

"Really?"

"Yep, you collect killers Mr Black, but Jimmy collects psychopath's, he calls them his no limits crew and they are, daddy has all the drugs and sweeties needed, get it?"

"Oh, yes son, I get it all, so he's well overdue then?"

Billy shrugged and smiled at him, "None of mine and all that boss!"

"Yes Billy, mine, I get that!"

"For the greater plan boss!"

"Yes, I get that as well!"

CHAPTER 20 ... PEARCE AND VIGO ... OFFICE OF CORPERATE LAW

They entered the swinging doors of the giant office complex, and Mr Black looked at the giant light box board with the names of the companies listed and what floor they were on, the people were like ants moving all over the place, no one even looked at them let alone stopped, Billy lost patience waiting for someone to speak to him, so he put him arm out and stopped a woman at the lifts.

"I am from mars, and I seek your leader!"

The tall woman looked down on him and laughed, and asked, "English?"

"Yes madam!"

"Funny accent, right?"

"Err ... it's how we're taught madam."

"Since when?"

"Well King John and the Magna Carta, and then in 1066 and all that as well, strange, eh?"

She focussed on him again, "Do you know Simon Peg from the Mission impossible franchise?"

"Yeah, a neighbour in Walthamstow, gay you know?"

"Is he? Oh, what a shame, and you?"

"Oh, much worse than that, married!"

"Is she's at home?"

"Yes, carving knife in hand if I play away, get me madam?"

"Yeah, I get you, err ......?"

"Billy and you?"

"Oh, I never give my name and number out on a first contact."

"A lawyer, eh?"

"Yeah, can you tell?"

"Oh, yeah, I can tell these things," he held the card in front of her face, "These blokes, where do I go darling?"

"Am I?"

"What, my darling?"

"Yeah, say you really are a forward guy, is that normal am I right?"

"Yes, you are!" he waved the card again.

"Oh, third floor end of the corridor, not nice folks like you, so what are you doing dealing with those guys?"

"A dirty job someone has to do, right?"

"Dirty?"

Billy thumbed to Mr Black as he fumed at the side of him.

"Bailiffs, tut, tut, eh?"

"What, bankruptcy?"

He raised his eyebrows and smiled at her "I have to go and drink my milk, sorry."

"Because you're a good boy, right honey?"

"I love American birds, so forward with whatever they want."

"And we're so helpful to lost English men who smell divine."

Mr Black has heard enough and dragged him into the open lift and pressed for the third floor, the lift doors closed, and another woman leaned into him the smell his aftershave.

"For the brave, just for the rutting season!" said Mr Grey.

She stepped away from him as doors pinged open, Mr Black giggled at his banter, then dragged him into the corridor to search for the office they wanted and pushed him along in silence.

Billy turned to him and did the zip it, let me do the talking mime across his lips, then he waited at the door for Mr Black to open it for him.

The door was opened, and he was pushed in, he smiled at the two secretary's working behind the chrome desks tapping away at their computers.

"What time is your appointment sirs?"

"An appointment, wow, what a good idea, yes I like that, so is he in?"

"He's in conference sir, sorry."

"Sorry for what, it's his fault not yours darling."

"He won't see you sir!"

"Why not, am I invisible or something?"

"Sir, he's in conference!"

Mr Back opened the door and waved for him to enter the office

Billy gave her the smile, "My bodyguard, he insists darling, sorry."

The men talking at the desk looked up to see the giant and the young man enter their office, Mr Black leaned into Billy's ear and whispered, "That's Bobby Vigo!"

Billy gave them the reassuring smile, then nodded to Mr Black,

"Good moaning chaps, how's everything hanging, good?"

Mr Black cornered Bobby by the chairs and grabbed him by the collar then dragged him to the window.

"Out that window I think Mr Black!"

Mr Black now had him by the hair and pushed to open the window, but it wouldn't budge.

"Child safety locks on all the window gentlemen, so no window jumpers today please," said the fat man at the desk.

"Well, how civilised, so you must be ......?"

"Alexander Pierce, senior partner and you sir are illegal in all of your movements!"

"Wow, a proper lawyer, I like that, so, who set us up then, you or him?"

"What, I don't understand the question young sir?"

"The reason Mr Black there is trying to kill Mr Vigo is that we were set up to be killed last night, not nice, not nice at all people, and some or our company want to slaughter you guys right here and now, Mr Black, will you please reel it in sir and be a bit more civilised?"

The fat, red faced gentleman still sitting at his desk stared at them in confused silence.

Billy waved his fingers in front of him, "Recognise any of my new rings gents?"

The fat man shook his head, but Bobby stared in horror at them.

"Ah, recognition, yes Mr Vigo, these are rings that used to belong to your best buddy Mr John Winstanley, now of course deceased, and swimming with the fish in the Hudson river!"

"No way!" said Bobby, "No Goddamned way man!"

Mr Black pushed Bobby down to sit in his seat.

"The TV please Mr Black, what time does the news come on lads?"

"All the time!"

"Good, turn it up please Mr Black, let's hear the latest."

He turned the volume up with the remote as they listened to the latest news, the picture came up with red alerts under the screen, warning viewer discretion is advised some pictures might be disturbing.

The announcer covered the removal of a naked man from the Hudson river this morning and a fireman turned the body over to reveal the face full on.

"We cannot identify the man found in the Hudson river this morning and police are asking for help in identification for viewers." said the announcer.

"The man has been stabbed through the mouth, tongue and upper pallet into his brain, and the murder was committed around midnight eastern time."

The second news item was the burnt-out top floor building in the city and piles of dead men in the foyer entrance, "One could literally walk on dead bodies to the lifts and rivers of blood flowed out into the car park, four men are being searched for in the incident and is believed to be gang related incident and for people to not panic at the scene, the police commissioner has said that they were Hispanic and carried high calibre machine guns, also mines were set in the lift shafts, leading to the bomb squad being called to the scene, the whole building is now cordoned off for public safety!"

Mr Black switched off the tv and stared at them in silence.

Billy grinned to Bobby Vigo who was now white faced with fear.

"A traitor to the cause and paid the price of upsetting Mr Black here."

The fat man tried to take his phone off the desktop, but Billy beat him to it, snatched it and put it in his pocket.

"What a great idea!" he searched his inside pocket and took out his own phone and placed it on the table for Mr Pierce to see what was on the screen.

The man stared in horror as Mr Red and Mr Blue were seating sandwiches in the upper part of the screen and on the main picture children were playing on the front lawn.

"Shit!" screeched Mr Pierce, "My God, my kids playing out front of the house, so what do you want, I'll do it, no matter, I'll do it!"

"Ok, clam please sir, let me explain what's happening here, Mr Black here sent two of his people to check you out sir, now, I'm new to this business, but Mr Black here and his crew are not, brutal people Mr Pierce, and very nasty at being betrayed like we were, both of those lads were wounded last night by Mr Winstanley, so they have anger management issues already, understand?"

"Anything, anything, just get me off the hook!" screamed the man.

"Calm sir, let me explain please, now do I need to go into the gruesome challenges of losing friends and relatives this way, do I?"

"No sir, you don't, but please don't hurt my kids, they're innocents in all this!"

"Funny that, because only a short while ago so was I, but your friends dragged me into it all, and I'm taking to it, I'm the brains, can you tell sir?"

"Anything, but we are protected, you must realise that sir."

"Not very well apparently, so, the house, not far from the river are you sir?"

"No, anything you want I can get it, give it, anything, just ask and it's yours!"

"Ok, calm please sir, I asked for this to demonstrate how really unprotected most of us are, "Mr Vigo here is in a similar situation and Mr Black wanted bodies floating down the river, so you two owe me for changing his mind on this, understand?"

"Yes, thankyou sir!"

"Information please?"

They looked at him in silence.

"Oh dear, silence is a dangerous thing gent's, his boys get real nasty very quickly, so nothing from you then?"

"Yes, what do you want, you got it! We'll make the deal, no matter what!" said Bobby Vigo.

"Good, so let me tell you our plan straight up, ok, now the owner of the lost finance is, well confused, right?"

"No, English bankers stole his money, I was there, and that big guy said he had them all and the money!"

"Ah, you see Mr Vigo, now there's the nub of our problem here, your memory and Mr Blacks backers, get it yet?"

"Get what sir?"

"The takeover, did you think that he believed it was the English who took his money, no, the Don is smarter than that, isn't he? So, he had people check it out, and that's why he fled to Miami, scared you see, he wanted a war but didn't want to start it, clear so far gentlemen?"

"But he?"

"He knew, right for the start that another family was muscling in on his domain, another Don, or rightly, our third-party Don in fact!"

"But Don Giancarlo wouldn't dare!"

"Ah, now a big mouth can get you killed sir, after all, this is not about money is it, it's about family pride and these Sicilian bloods, get it?"

"Some slight way back when, well who knows with these people, an uncle got the chop by whoever, look, you know how it goes, but this is not about them really, this is about survival, understand?"

"Yes sir, so what is it you want us to do?"

"Well, you have a bigger problem that us, we are simply contractors for a third party, nothing more, so my job is to save lives, now you have a genuine Brith Gangster coming your way and he wants what he's owed, that's 50 mills, got that?"

"But we don't have that kind of money sir!"

"Yes, we'll get to that in a moment, and the bung owed to you as well, but the problem here is that he's a savage, I mean the real thing, so you have to play for time, just say they went that a way, and keep him and his boys calm, clear?"

"But we don't know the man or why he wants any money from us?"

"Ok, look, our third party hasn't shown respect, you know how it goes, right, so all you have to do is give him the 50 mill and he'll happily walk away satisfied."

"But from where?"

"The Dons money, the rest of it in your trust lockers, yes?"

"But he'll kill us!"

"He won't get the chance lads because he is soon to be laid to rest get me?"

"He's going to die?"

"Yeah, some sudden impact accident, I haven't worked out the details just yet, but Mr Black here and his mates are now moving down to Florida, contact work, you get everywhere these days, so the Don's money will be in your hands, so take 50 mill and give it to the ugly Englishman when he asks, ok, with that idea?"

"You are crazy, he will kill us all."

"Oh, I forgot to say that our third-party paymaster wants total annihilation, not one stone laid upon another, the old Roman way, not one wall or stone above ground and all his dependents, annihilation, the old Roman empire, not lost on some is it sir?"

"But that's impossible!"

"Is it? Well, you will see, now when the old man bites the dust, now that's your time to take a bite and run, ok? Best keep up with the news from down south."

"But we can't do that?"

"Oh, and another thing, in regard to any money the Don has in your influence, just lose it!"

"But we can't do that!"

"It's a bit repetitive around here Mr Black! Perhaps your alternative plan must come forward and our man wipes the bank clean, what do you think?"

Mr Black nodded to him in silence.

"No, no, don't do that please!"

"So let me make this very clear once and for all, or Mr Black and his associates might join your labour day Barbi and blacken your burgers, our third party wants complete silence in regards to any of the old Dons finances, your retirement in fact, look, let me ley this on the line so you understand our employer, he doesn't want a comeback from this, no dirty back stabbing vendetta's rolling on and on, get me here gents, the old man made enemies all over the place, not a peacemaker was he, it's about families in the end isn't it?

"Ok, I'm done here any quick questions because a fancy a big mack meal."

"You mentioned a bung, sir?"

"Ah, yes, look when the old man is no more, 50 mill for the bloke and 50 mill for you, you simply take the money and run, struth, do I have to all the thinking round here?"

He thumbed to the door and Mr Black opened it for him and he walked out

He smiled at the girls as he held his hands in the air, "Sorry, I have this thing about germs, good day all!" Mr Black opened the outer door for him, and they were gone.

On the way down Mr Black burst out laughing, "Now who do I work for again?"

Billy grinned at him in silence

"And who the hell is the third party?"

"Smoke and mirrors Mr Black, just smoke and mirrors."

"And the bloke crossing the Atlantic as we speak Mr Grey?"

"Well, not my department Mr Black, I am strictly logical planning and logistical support!"

"Mine then?"

"Well, der, Mr Black!"

"And Frank?"

"Oh, he takes up the crown, cars become just a sideline, a little like retirement, he'll like that!"

"My God, what have I done to let you loose in our world?"

"Did you get the name he mentioned Mr Black?"

"Yes, the Giancarlo family."

"King makers again, good all round, perhaps call in for a cash top up collection point?"

Mr Black growled at him to shut up as they walked out into the street, "Just point and let me shoot the bugger, I've got a headache! But why all this in the first place, couldn't we have just shot them and burnt the building to the ground?"

"Such unnecessary violent, fear Mr Black, fear is a better tool than a body down the river, the potential of their own body down the river is better."

"Psychology, eh?"

"Is that what it's called then boss?"

"You've just invented it haven't you sonny?"

"Have I?"

"Get in the bloody car and shut up!"

Mr Black sat in the driver's seat and smiled at Mr Grey, "Now listen very carefully because I will say this only once!"

"But without the bad French accent, eh?"

"Shut up and listen, I'm dropping you of at the airport, you are going to Miami, where Mr Pink will pick you up and take you to the lads who are in their planning stage, you can input if you like but listen Mr Grey, nothing fancy, simple is best, understand?"

"Oh, absolutely boss, simple is best, I might make that my new moto, yes, clear!"

He took a second look at Billy thinking he was making fun of him but realised that he was serious, and his planning had already started.

Mr Black was on the phone and speaking to his colour men, "I need work doing gentlemen, so up and at em please, and I care about war wounds? So, planning in one hour!"

Billy looked at him and smiled.

"What?"

"None of my business boss, but please make it terminal, because we can do without a London vendetta in the mix!"

"Shut up!"

CHAPTER 21 ... JFK AIRPORT ... ARRIVALS LOUNGE ... NEW YORK.

Mr Red in his Red polo neck jumper pulled up to his chin to cover the neck bandage waited at the end of the customs hall the other side of the big plastic screen.

He watched the chaos as the Brits were moved from one desk to another as they and their luggage were vigorously searched but nothing found.

Mr Red held his sign in the air and waited, he hoped they would understand the call, British archaeology group conference.

A large shadow blocked out natural light from the windows at the side of him and a monster peered down, "Speak English mate?"

He looked up to the face, "Yes, English born and bred!"

The man signalled to fellow monsters, and he was suddenly surrounded, "Welcome to the big apple folks!"

"Yuck!" said the big man, "I hate fruit!"

A wide fat man strutted down to them and stared at him, "Is this him Sick note?"

The classic flat cap and a cigar sticking out of the side of his mouth, he went to light it, but a uniformed officer pointed to the sign above them.

"Bloody yanks, all this poncy clean air crap!"

"Yes boss, and he wears the colours." said another big man.

"Another crappy idea, so who are you sonny?"

"Mr Red sir, I am your transport, Mr Black sent me as a courtesy."

"Thommy Bloodworth, so another stupid name then?"

"A system sir!"

"Bollocks to his bastard system, ok, move your arse, let's get this collecting visit done, the lads want to go to Disney in Florida, ever been?"

"Err ... no sir."

"Come with us if you like son?"

"No sir, working and all that."

"For Tommy Bloodworth then?"

"My boss sir."

"Boss my arse, and there's another fucker who owes me a very large drink."

"He'll meet you later sir, if that's ok?"

"In my own time sonny, let's not got excited, so take me to these bankers in the city, let's get the convo started, know anything about all this?"

Jimmy the saw walked off not bothering to have his answer, Mr Red walked faster to get to the minibus before his clients and opened all the doors.

"Well?" asked Jimmy, in his face.

"Err no sir, just a grunt on the line sir!"

"Done time I hear?"

"I was framed sir!"

Jimmy burst out laughing at him, "Same old crap then sonny?"

Jimmy sat behind him in the bus and asked question after question about his work.

"Confidential sir, I can't talk about any of our work, sorry!" he said it repeatedly.

"Not a bad policy really Mr Red, so he keeps a tight ship then?"

"Very sir."

He watched Jimmy and his boys in the mirror as he drove them into the big city, and he realised that the man had done his homework on Mr Black and was intending to tackle him on the touchy subject of money and knew how that convo would end.

"Earns big does he, with his Government contracts?"

"Not my department sir."

Jimmy laughed out loud, his boys joined in, Mr Red listened to the banter as he drove on into the big city centre.

"We're in a red zone now sir, no parking and not even stopping is allowed, so I have to drop you off and go round the block for your pickup, will you be long sir?"

"Same as London now then?"

"Worse, they tow away quicker here and the fee is a grand to get the vehicle back sir?"

"A great scam when you think of it, Government backed in fact, I might have to get into that game, we'll see how we go!"

"Through the government sir?"

"Well Tommy boy has links, don't he?"

"Yes sir, but I don't think he will like the idea."

"He'll do as he's bloody told as always, and pay his subs as always, so he's a millionaire I hear?"

"No in my knowledge group sir!"

"Oh, he's trained you well hasn't he boy?"

Mr Red stopped on double red lines in front of the office block, behind the white sedan, "Everyone out here please!"

The horns of the cars and taxi's hooted as Jimmy and his team got out of the bus, slowly, one or two of the drivers making all the noise receive stares from Jimmy's people.

"One hour sir, I'll be here for the pickup, ok with that?"

Jimmy ignored him as he lit his cigar and walked off, the rest of them followed on in silence.

The rear brake light flashed from the sedan in front of him, so he pulled off and followed it around the corner to side entrance to the block and parked up again, the brake light flashed four time and Mr Red knew the trap was about to be sprung, he gave Mr Blue a quick flash of his head lights and waited for the inevitable noise to start.

Mr Blue winked at him in his mirror before starting his engine up again, Mr Red followed his pattern and did the same.

Within seconds the whole area was in total meltdown and the sound of a machine gun echoed out and into the street, Mr Red pulled off slowly at a walking pace as silence descended over the buildings.

Mr Red followed on as a blocking vehicle if there was trouble and slowly came to a stop, then watched the large figure walking out of the building, the over coat flapping in the breeze, Mr Black with the woolly hat pulled down and over his recognisable hair, he stepped into the sedan and was driven away, Mr Red followed on as a blocking vehicle with his minibus in case of an emergency until they reached the freeway, when he overtook their car and headed for the river to dump the cases and burn out the minibus.

All the time the whooping of police and ambulances echoed in the streets as they flashed past in the opposite direction.

Two hour later Mr Red stood on a street corner eating a local chilli dog and gasping with the heat of the thing, a white sedan pulled up at the side of him and the driver laughed as the window was buzzed down, "Just imagine what that thing is doing to your innards, burns in and burns out Mr Red?"

Mr Red dropped the molten hotdog in a trash can and got into the car to sit beside Mr Black, who was silently reading the account's so far of the contract.

"And do not breathe over me please, bloody disgusting food they have around here!"

Mr Blue stared into the interior mirror to gauge what mood the old man was in, Mr Red winked back at him in silence.

"How the hell can he spend half a mill on equipment, what the hell's wrong with these people?"

"Expenses boss?"

"There are expenses and there's taking the piss, what the hell are they doing down there?"

Mr Blues mouth asked the question automatically and he regrated asking just as quickly as Mr Black gave him the stare to shut the fuck up.

"Airport boss?" asked Mr Blue.

Mr Black nodded in silence, but Mr Blue wanted an answer to a burning question and glared at Mr Red to ask it.

At this, Mr Red coughed then asked, "Old job done now then boss?"

"Yes, I will not forgive or forget injustice on me and mine, you can pass that on if you like!"

"Yes sir."

Mr Red winked at him again in the mirror with thanks.

"So, are we all flying today boss?"

"No, just me gentlemen, you pair drive, a nice restful cruise down south with all the kit you need, almost a holiday, but for the fact that we need you in Miami in three days for the final actions, contract rules apply gentlemen, and they are?" he asked.

"No birds, drink or trouble Mr Black." Said Mr Red

"Walk away from trouble and association is a sin."

Mr Blue looked at him in confusion, but Mr Red glared at him to ask.

"In what way boss?"

Trouble follows some people, the bad girl, the drunk the troublemaker, avoid all please, because it will all be your fault if it kicks off, clear?"

"Yes boss."

"And no pissing about, and to be on time?"

"One has to be early sir!" said Mr Red.

Ok, let me out here."

Mr Blue stopped the car and let Mr Black take his overnight bag and walk off without saying another word.

They watched him enter the flight terminal and disappear in the crowd.

"So, what the hell was that all about Red?"

"A very old grudge, planned by Mr Grey, so what do you think?"

"Why here and why now though, Blue boy?"

"Mr Greys planning, wow, eh?"

"He'll get us all killed though, he's not right in the head, is he?"

"And we are?"

"Ah, yes, a good point, and did you hear how he changed their hearts and mind?"

Mr Blue shook his head.

"He introduced fear into their brains, he stopped them at source, clever right?"

"But they will always be the leak though Mr Blue boy."

"Doing my head in Red man!"

He pulled off and headed back to the freeway, a change of vehicle coming up Blue boy, come on take a guess."

"A boat?"

"And you would risk your life in that ocean out there?"

"Yeah, why not?"

Drowned eaten by sharks now what, Mr Red,"

"Wimpy!"

"Carrot top!"

"Blue nose!"

"How did you know that?"

"What?"

"That I supported Leicester city."

"Ah, that's why I don't like you then, you're a midland pie eater!"

"Yes, and a proud eater of pork pies! And what the hell is that?" he pointed to the wreck of a van.

Mr Red pulled up to the campervan and smiled at him in the back, "Cover, we're a gay couple heading for the sunny vacation, so start loading up."

"And the gunshot wounds?"

"Well victims of racism, obviously, err der!"

"So, who's the effeminate one?"

"Well, I thought it would be you, the unshaven he man of the team."

Mr Blue scratched his head with his middle finger in the usual insult "Ok, lets load up moron!"

"Yes darling! And besides, I have a bad leg, remember?"

CHAPTER 22 ... KEY LARGO ... FLORIDA STATE.

Billy had his feet in the water off the sea wall and watched the little fish nibbling at the hard skin of his toes, Mr Pink watched him with interest, "You are bonkers!"

"What, it's free mate, what can I say here?"

"Well, you can start with a basic plan before the old man descends on us and starts all the shouting!"

Billy had lost focus on Mr Pink and watched the giant low loaders rumble down the distant freeway carrying their heavy loads, "What are they?"

Mr Pink looked round to see what he was looking at and the slow-moving convoy of heavy loaded trucks rumbling along.

"From the quarry, the biggest they do apparently."

"What are?"

"Caterpillar D11's, the real monsters of the quarry world, the bucket alone can lift ten tons in one go, impressive, eh?"

"Oh yes, very impressive, so much so, that I want to but one."

"What, but why?"

"No, change that to two, yes two monsters, now I like that plan!"

"What bloody plan."

"The ever so simple plan Mr Pink, so who would be selling those?"

"Err ... State road services, so what?"

"Ok, Mr Pink, get them on the phone please."

"What, now?"

"Yes, now please and get me a price."

Mr Pink scrambled for his phone and punched in the state road services, he flicked the pages one by one as Mr Grey carried on getting his toes manicured for free.

"Oh, a sad day in the office Mr Grey, they're going bust, they've lost their Government contract so that's them going for scrap!"

"Scrap, oh, do me a favour, get on the line and find out how much."

"How much for what?"

"The lot, tools, kit, road signs, whatever, but mostly our new bull dozers!"

"But they might be knackered?"

"Well, we'll repair them then, some of us are mechanics Mr Pink!"

Mr Pink stared with an open mouth as he watched Mr Greys brain working.

Mr Grey nodded again, "Come on, chop, chop, find out how much."

Mr Pink was now on the phone as he conversed with someone down the line.

Mr Grey was also on the line to Sandra, "Hello Babe, all right, are you?"

"And where the bloody hell have you been you knob, the media is going bonkers over there, some nutter is killing everyone, now that's not you, is it Billy?"

"Na, I'm in Key Largo, and it's wonderful, feet in the sea, just missing my babe, that's all."

"Oh, you sweet little ponce, so Its business then?"

"Logistics babe, I need to make a cash transfer, I'm buying a road repairs company over here."

"How much and why Billy?"

"Well just an idea, investments and all that, look, we have to splash it about, don't we?"

"So, a plant hire company?"

"Err no babe hold on, I'll give you a figure in a second," he turned to Mr Pink and smiled.

Mr Pink had found the company and was now on the phone, "So, I have a British investor on the line Larry, and he's very interested in the whole company, yes, everything, but especially including the D11's, between you and me Larry I think he's a bit of a train spotter, get my meaning here?"

"Billy held the mouthpiece in his phone and whispered "Total, I need a total, cash draft today GMT time, yes?"

Mr Pink carried on with his conversation.

"Err Larry, he's very excited to be buying your company, so can you give me a round figure please, yes, lock stock and bins, everything, yes, oh, and your and ongoing contracts, yes, he's a cash buyer Larry, so strike while the irons cold right?"

"Ah hot, yes, ok, got the total yet? Ok, he's here with me, I'll tell him, hold the line please."

"Two million!"

Billy nodded and returned to his phone call, "Yes babe, so I need two mills transferred over here to buy this company, a bargain apparently, cool, eh?"

"If we're investing in America Billy I need a company name, do you have one for us?"

"Err yes babe, give me five." He held the hand over the phone again and pointed to the fish nibbling his toes, "What are they Mr Pink?"

Mr Pink held the line on his phone and looked at what he was looking at, "Err Zebra fish, little guys, they clean sharks and that, oh and turtles when they get the chance."

"He went back to his call, "Yes Larry, he's agreed to the price and is contacting his bank in the UK right now for a transfer, are you ready for that?"

"Yes Sand, the new company is called Zebra investments, out of London of course, got that, oh, I'll ask babe hold the line." What's his company called?"

Yes sir, he's just asking what the name of your company is, we like to use familiar local name if you understand sir."

He held the line again and whispered to Billy.

"Key West Road repairs, and plant hire!"

Billy nodded to him in thanks, "Key west road repairs and plant hire, got that?"

"Billy, I need numbers numbollocks!"

"Ah, I'll pass you over to Mr Pink babe."

"Who the hell is he Billy?"

"A friend dear and our new road repair contracts manager." He handed the phone over to Mr Pink who was dumbstruck, at his new title, "Really?"

"Yes, really, really mate, ok, get it done!"

"Ok, Larry, deal done, I'm going to pass you over to our London accountant for the final financial agreement and of course the payment."

He closed his call and Billy passed him his phone with a grin.

Sandra was now in his ear, "Ok bollock brain pass him over, and how much did he want for it?"

"Err .... two million Ma'am."

"Who the hell does he think he's dealing with here? I'll chug him down a little for being a cash buyer, and did you say they were almost bankrupt, so give me his number and let me sort this!"

"I've pinged it to you Ma'am."

"Yes ok, but any idea why Billy wants this busted company?"

"Plans of mice and men Ma'am!"

"Rats more like!" she closed the call, and he felt the draft in his ear.

"Ok, Mr Pink, a good day's work," he was looking and searching a map on his phone, "And look at that." Billy passed over his phone again for Mr Pink to look at the map.

Mr Pink looked at it and smiled but he didn't understand why he was looking at a random spot on a map.

Billy snatched it back and widened the picture then upped the scale to reveal the whole county.

Mr Pink still didn't get it.

"The roadies stock yard and trailer camp, where all the gear is stored?"

Mr Pink shook his head again.

"And a great big hacienda down the road, a wonderful desolation site, don't you think?"

Mr Pinks eyes sparkled as he realised a little of the plan in Billy's head, "So our new base of operations, yes?"

"Yes, until the others have studied the routines and timings of the target, good for you Mr Pink?"

"Just perfect Mr Grey, but the cash outlay is going to give Mr Black a heart attack."

"Na, It'll come off his tax entitlement, so I want you to run the site, ok?"

"Err .... Yeah! Hold up, did you say it's from his tax payments?"

Billy suddenly pulled his feet out of the water, "Look at that, that little swine just drew blood on my big toe!"

Mr Pink couldn't help laughing at the day he was having with this lunatic who had just bought a company unseen and paid two million for it, he looked at his watch, "And all that action to buy the place Mr Grey, in less than fifteen minutes!"

"Was it really?"

"Yes boss, really, really!"

CHAPTER 23 ... MIAMI INTERNATIONAL AIRPORT ... TAXI RANK.

Mr Black walked out of the air-cooled airport into a 40% heatwave hitting Miami, it felt like he had just entered a baking over and he was the hot pie placed on a breathless shelf, he scanned the yellow cabs on the rank for a colour, a bright yellow ping pong ball on the top of a roof aerial gave away the one he needed to get into.

He opened the door and sat down in the cool, climate-controlled cab, "Is it normally this hot around here, Mr Yellow?"

"A little heat wave boss!"

"Talking of heat waves, where is that little shit?"

"Err ... I'll let him explain sir, but he has gone over the top a little, still we have a legitimate base of operations at least." He handed him an equipment list together with the estimated price of it all.

Mr Black stared then counted the equipment down the list with the grand total making him cough, "What the hell is that lunatic doing, three million?"

"He calls it future investments boss."

"And he has a plan at the end of this?"

"Oh, yes boss, simple he says!"

"And that means what?"

"Oh, you just have to listen to this one boss, so simple its bordering on either genius or he's flipped his lid."

"And your opinion on the plan, Mr Yellow?"

"Oh, a definite genius boss!"

Mr Black turned the paper over and studied the research done on the target, "Timings?"

"Observed over three days Mr Black, an iron routine Mr Brown tells me, and he calls it Fort Knox, gun emplacements, sniper overcover towers, iron gratings and possibly even land minds, he's not quite sure about that and is checking it out as we speak, he's wearing the uniform you see."

"What bloody uniform?"

"Oh, the company uniform, Key West, Road repairs and Plant hire, it even has the state badge on the pocket, very colourful sir, he's doing ground research on the road repairs due to be done soon and took the time to talk to the lads on the gate, they gave him a cold beer to sooth his sweaty brow!"

"And his opinion?"

"A very strong defence then?"

"Oh, he's right sir, we'll drive by on the way to our base, and you can check it out."

"And our weaponry?"

"Small arms only Mr Black, we didn't want to stir up local suspicion trying to by big guns and ammunition and all that."

"Good lad, very wise, ok, take me there please," Mr Black had to roll over and sleep from the flight and the previous night's work."

"Is New York ok, sir?"

"Why ask son?"

"Well, the tv news has been blasting all day and night about fires and sudden deaths, English men they say, we were worried sir."

"Na, someone just evening up the scores, oh, by the way, Mr Blue and Mr Red have been wounded, so we need to rethink assignments when they get here, sitting jobs perhaps?"

"In the NYC action sir?"

"Yes, and Mr Driver is no longer with us, he sleeps with the fishes!" he watched Mr Yellows eyes in the mirror.

"I smell betrayal in there, sir?"

"I knew you were quick Mr Yellow and yes, he had a very clever double bubble payment system in place, and we were going to be the freebies, sacrificed for his third-party supporter, but we pre-empted his ambitions and terminated his employ in that matter."

Mr Yellow watched him again in the mirror, "With your primary weapon we were told sir."

"What a big mouth Mr Grey has young man!"

"But we are brethren sir!"

Mr Black blinked and then smiled at him, "Yes, sorry kid, we are brethren, and we watch each other's back."

"And you took time to save Red and Blue?"

"Yes son, it doesn't mean I actually like them, it's the brethren commitment, obviously!"

"Yes Mr Black, obviously!"

Mr Yellow smiled at him in the mirror again, but Mr Black was now asleep on the back seats.

He continued to watch him in the mirror from time to time and drove on to the freeway to their new base of operations, he felt better, because with the old man in the chair they would all feel better, regardless of Mr Greys hair brained scheme, the uniting of the brethren always felt good, for all of them.

CHAPTER 24 ... FLORIDA STATE HIGHWAY ... ROAD CONSTRUCTION SITE.

Mr Black woke when the road surface made the car tumble from side to side.

"What the hell is this Mr Yellow?"

"Needs resurfacing sir."

"But why?"

"Well because the lads have stripped off the tarmac."

"What, they've been doing civil engineering and road re-surfacing?"

"Yes sir, cover for the job."

Mr Black gave him the eyes of discontent before looking at the target mansion off the main highway, "Is that it?"

"Yes, more of as housing complex, Mr Brown talks to them most days, making friends and all that."

"And he studies the defences while he's there, right?"

"Right sir."

"So how far are we away from here?"

"Five miles down the road."

"That's good then and who planned this?"

Mr Yellow grinned in the mirror to him.

"Mr Grey then?"

Mr Yellow nodded.

"So, any other surprises?"

Mr yellow giggled and looked away before he burst out laughing.

Mr Black knew that there was a problem, his problem was, that he had let loose a stark raving lunatic for his planning and he dreaded to hear the crazy plan that was going to hit him when he arrived at the site.

Mr Yellow had slowed down to give Mr Black a look at the fortress, and he now realised that he was not interested in anything more than just the plan.

"Have they had a meeting of the planners committee?"

"Yes boss."

"And?"

Mr Yellow burst out laughing, he couldn't control the funny look on Mr Blacks confused face and that made it even funnier.

"Oh, just get me there!"

Mr Yellow slowed down as they arrived at the construction site, to allow Mr Black to read the words on the contractor's notification board out front.

Mr Black read it out loud, "Welcome to Florida highways road construction, your friendly Roadies, we make it for your safety, please be patient with our people and safety first."

"No high viz vest, no steel toe capped boots = no job!"

"What the hell is he doing?"

"Cover colourations he calls it boss."

Mr Yellow parked the taxi as Mr Black looked round the site, and as he got out, what initially looked like a coloured wall was in fact a massive machine, he looked up to the cab the to the wheels and tires taller than him, "What the hell is this?" he screeched out to whoever was listening to him.

Mr Green approached smiling, "The Caterpillar D11 sir, the biggest they do!"

"For why?"

Mr Green pointed to a dust cloud on the horizon, "Mr Grey sir is road testing the offensive weapon of choice, he left these for you sir, for when you arrive, he suggests you join him over in the swamp over there for a brief of his new and very simple plan."

Mr Black tutted in frustration, "And you morons let him spend three million on this place?"

"The plan sir, and we voted on it."

"And?"

"Unanimous vote, all agreed sir!" he handed over the little key for the monster and pointed for the step to climb into the cab, then walked away giggling.

Mr Black grunted and climbed up to the cab of the monster, it was like sitting on top of the world, his view of the world changed as he tried to find the keyhole and starter button.

"On the floor!" shouted Mr Green, "Near the brake."

Mr Black gave him a nod of thanks then started up the massive engine and gave it a couple of revs, then put it in gear and put his foot down, the monster rattled on, and he found it very easy to steer with the power steering and power brakes.

He headed for the dust cloud on the horizon and Billy going round and round in another D11.

Billy was concentrating of his gear changes and wondered why it was so complex, then realized again that the thing was like this because it was so very monstrous and could be very dangerous in the wrong hands, it made him think and laugh because he was just that, the wrong hands.

Another shadow parked up at the side of him and he had to give Mr Black the toothy grin, he could see he was swearing at him through the glass then gave him the sign to kill the engine.

Suddenly there was silence, and he climbed out onto the tracks to speak to Mr Black.

"Well, you said simple so here it is, simple!"

"Three million pounds simple?"

"Cover, we needed cover, good, eh?"

Mr Black had to nod and even laugh at the mad man, "So it was you who ripped up the road then?"

"Oh, yes, just familiarising the locals to our project."

"The roads?"

"Yes, the roads."

"So, the plan it what?"

Billy grinned, "We run them over!"

"Hold up, I thought you said to run them over?"

"I did Mr Black, we simply roll up and run them over, what could be simpler than that?"

Mr Black stared at the madman for a second or two before he burst out laughing.

"With these monsters?"

"Yes sir, with these D11's the biggest that Caterpillar do, what do you think?"

"That you are bonkers, is what it think!"

"But you said simple, so this is simple."

"And if they shoot the driver in the head from long distance, then what?"

"Well, that's your side of the planning Mr Black!"

Mr Black sat and stared at him as he milled over the plan in his head, the target site, the two monsters and the potential dangers of just showing up and to drive over the targets.

"Ok, potentially good, let me discuss this with Mr Blue and Mr Red when they arrive."

"And the driving of the D11, is it good?"

"Yes, surprisingly good, but not secure from flying bullets, that's the problem, yes?"

"Yes boss, agreed! So do you need more practice?"

"No Mr Grey, so have you estimated how long it will take to reach the target site?"

"An hour we think."

Billy stood up and returned to the cab, he started the engine up again and pulled off to return to the base.

Mr Black instantly knew it was a race as Billy put his foot down, so he did the same and followed him along the track they had created alone the sides of the marshland.

They raced neck and neck along the marshes, maxed out and 20 miles per hour, Mr Black overtook him and grinned then beat him to the imaginary line on the service road near the portacabins.

He was given a round of applause by the lads who were watching the action, when both drivers jumped down Mr Black took Mr Gey in a head lock and marched off the food cabin.

"And anyway, Mr Grey you are not driving that thing, what if you're killed, do we still get paid?"

"Yes boss, "said Billy from under Mr Blacks armpit, "She'll fume and swear, and it'll be your fault of course, but she will pay up, after all this is a job and she pays for jobs!"

Mr Black let him go, but what he wanted had been said, no one had asked the obvious question until now, he looked around at the expectant faces, "Question asked gentlemen, ok now?"

They knew that he had understood their mood and nodded to his answer and then walked off to do other jobs.

He waved over Mr Green, "Ok, Mr Greys idea is sound, but these things are not used to being fired on, so do something about defending the drivers please, front and rear, perhaps ever a rear gunner for when we turn, yes?"

"Yes boss, I'll use some of those body armour pack, it's a big Ned Kelly like though?"

"Ned Kelly is good, just do what you can with what you have a bit of steel plate here and there, I can ask no more Mr Green so get it done please!"

Mr Pink came over and handed him his high viz vest and a hard hat in bright yellow, then smiled, Mr Black thumbed to the gate and all signage, "Yes sir, site regulations please."

"For cover?"

"Health and safety sir!"

Mr Black grabbed his arm and squeezed, "And you plan to run this company afterwards?"

"Yes sir, I'm inspired by Mr Greys offer and trust."

"But this place will explode with interest when we've done here son, you do understand that?"

Mr Pink smiled at his lack of understanding of the plan.

"There will be no one left sir, his plan is to dissolve that place into the environment, not one brick laid upon another, this is not only annihilation this is desolation as in the Roman army way of treating enemies, a total destruction, just like Carthage, never to recover, never, just an overgrown smear of marshland, get it?"

Mr Black listened, then turned to see Mr Grey laughing with the colour men as they laughed at him at being under Mr Black's armpit.

"My God, what a monster we work for Mr Pink!"

Mr Pink turned with him and shared the look, "Will this work though boss?"

Mr Black started laughing, "I said to him, make it simple, not of your complex third-party crap, just bloody simple!"

"And it is bloody simple sir, right?"

"Well, I've never done this before Mr Pink, so don't ask me, ask that moron over there."

"Are we under the influence of a genius sir?"

"Yes, son afraid so! Well, I'm hungry, what's for dinner? And none of that local chilli crap, my guts can't take that stuff, clear?"

"Spag boll?"

Mr Blacks face betrayed his English taste buds as he scowled.

"I'll put you a couple of jacket spuds in sir, cheese and coleslaw topping perhaps?"

He received Mr Blacks best smile, "Good lad, you know my English tastes lad."

"Or perhaps a Yorkshire pudding with sausage and gravy inside it?"

Mr Black lifted him up and carried him on his shoulders over to the cook house container to get it started as the lads laughed watching the scene.

As he waited in the canteen container a map with unrolled in front of him on the long table, by Mr Brown, he placed the salt pots in the corners to stop it moving.

Mr Brown pointed to the target with a spoon, "Ok, the target hacienda complex, I think over six buildings, the mandatory swimming pool and outer buildings the suit, but they also have an armoury and a full-sized target range, indoors."

"We think it is the long building to the back of the main house, note the house has only two stories, we feel that it lacked planning permission for anything bigger due to the natural drainage of the land, and also feel that it won't have any cellars for the same reason, it's a flood plain in the natural world, they shouldn't have built on the place in the first place."

"But he wanted a vantage point, and a place purpose built for his team, right?" said Mr Black.

"Yes boss, and he has the power to do what he likes, so a basic mistake from the start."

"So, we could possibly press the whole place into the swamp?"

"I feel that the place has been built on a natural sand bank, and that's with all its shifting sand problems, so built originally with plenty of ground concrete or pile driven posts with steel reenforced structure work before the brick build was started."

"And guard towers?"

"Just made of scaffolding, a dog on a lead could pull them over, not a problem."

"But they could snipe at us from there, correct?"

"Well, during my conversation with various guards I find that they are not used, well only for lighting when they have special visitors, there is a platform there but hard to climb up to, so they don't bother."

"Ah, visitors, when do they have visitors?"

"Well once a week they have a bus load of tarts driven in to entertain the troops, local girls apparently, I was even invited to a party if I wanted."

"But you declined right?"

"Yes boss, contract rules and all that."

"Good lad, so, the bottom line, how many are there at any one time, and is that all of them?"

"Funny you should ask that one sir, on labour day they have a big old cook out shindig, they invited us in fact, that's if we like."

"So, friends then?"

"Yes sir, just grunts on the wrong side, that's it really."

"And on labour day they would have the girls arrive, yes?"

"We assume, sir."

"Ok, good, a good report Mr Brown, well done, and are they familiar in any way to the D11's?"

"Well, we rumbled past a few times to scrape the road surface away and blocked the road to normal traffic, they have limited road access when we put the traffic lights in, we can control movement if required."

"Oh, very impressive Mr Brown, ok, that's the day then, or the early morning after, would be better, yes? And will all his people be there?"

"We think so sir, a big family shindig for the lads, women and drink sir, it might be the death of them, right?"

"Children?"

"None seen or heard sir, a bachelor pad on a big scale I think."

"Oh, yes Mr Brown, it will be the death of them! So, they might be slow to recognise a threat to life then?"

"Yes boss, friends coming to the party and all that."

"Good, ok, continue with your surveillance and keep tabs on visitors, we need to count numbers of shooters, clear?"

"Clear sir!"

Mr Pink proudly placed the plate in front of him for his approval, "You like sir?"

"Mmmm." was the only sound out of Mr Black.

Mr Grey came and sat down next to him as he ate, "Northern food is that?"

"Mmm." said Mr Black.

"What is it, bangers in cake and gravy?"

"Umm." said Mr Black, but his eyes said sod off while I'm eating.

"He does a great chilli con you know?"

"Mmmm."

"Should I leave you alone to eat sir?"

"Mmmmm!" but the look said go away or I might have to shoot you.

The scraping of the plate signalled the assembly, and all sat down to wait his decision on the attack.

He had finally finished a took a swig of water as he focused on them.

"Plan, plan, plan, plan!" was the echo around the room as focused again.

"Ok, give it a rest, we're not a bloody glee club, ok, to the plan, yes, I agree, simple, direct and bloody stupid, but we have here a tough nut of a compound, they have hidden shooter slots, and overcover points if needed, the only thing we have in our favour is shear surprise, they won't expect nutters to attack with great big bull dozers, what a bloody stupid idea?"

"We must assume that the gate guards have direct connection the main house and gunmen can come running to help in any attack, we have to also assume that they have immediate access to mortars and rockets, all the American kit, so we have to be sharp and ruthless in taking down sudden targets."

"We have a date, and that's labour day, well not the day, obviously, we have the night and early morning after, sleepy boozed up enemies with headaches and bad moods, well we can sort that for them, and give them the good news eh, lads?"

The place erupted in cheering and screeching, but he shut them down with a wave.

"Ok, work to do, Mr Brown will continue surveillance and get a greater understanding of how they live and work, deliveries for food from shops, cooking and feeding times, leisure times, they have a pool, lucky sods!"

"Ok, weaponry, we need snipers to surround the compound and to take down any face that looks like it could hold and fire a weapon, ruthless please, everyone, clear?"

"Once the D11's roll up, their time is very short, they will panic, and as we always say, panic is good, their panic will kill them."

"Talking of the tractors, they need protection from long shots from the house and I'm looking forward to the sight of our new Ned Kelly D11's, all clad in fancy armour, we need the electric cannons to be bolted to the rear buckets for a rear gunner."

"As you have all probably heard, Mr Red and Mr Blue were wounded in our last action, we were betrayed gentlemen and it has its price, so Mr Driver sleeps with the fishes, well perhaps by now in the county morgue where betrayers belong, so when Blue and Red show up they are obvious candidates for rear gunners in the D11's, one cannot just swan around pretending to be in pain in front of the lads, right?

The place erupted in laughing at his statement and all understood the responsibility of being a colour man.

"Ok, gentlemen, any obvious questions or potential new ideas for the plan?"

A hand razed at the end of the table, "Yes Mr Purple!"

"Sir, we hear that you didn't really trust Mr Driver and so you were ready for his betrayal, could you elaborate on that for us, after all he supplied the weapons, we don't get it?"

"Look out of our mouths comes part of our character, a deceiver, a liar, and a cheat, as part of yours and indeed my education, we have to notice these things, I simply listened to his plan and it seemed bad to my sensibilities, his plan was to snuff out sub-contractors to keep the secret, now that would have been a very bad contractor practice, he would have laid himself and us open to hostile engagements from other contractors, do you see the fairness here gentlemen?"

"We have a responsibility to be professional in all our work, both big jobs and small jobs, clear Mr Purple?"

"Yes sir, and is it right that you rescued both Red and Blue from inevitable execution by unknowns?"

"Yes, Mr Grey did the driving and got us out of there very quickly, but look, our real power is in our loyalty to each other, our Brethren are closer than family, no one else cares gentlemen, only your Brethren who protects your back as you ......?"

"Protect his!" shouted the audience.

"With your primary weapon Mr Black?"

Mr Black flicked his wrist and produced his number one Sikes dagger from his strapped-on sleeve sheath, "Our last line of defence gentlemen, we must win in all contacts, we do not lose a fight with them!"

He thumbed to the outside world, "They don' understand the need for us, they don't get it at all, but we are Brethren to the bones, yes?"

"To the bones!" shouted the Brethren as one.

Billy looked on and felt a pride in being allowed into their world and to be excepted by them as a planner.

"Ok, Periwinkle and I will be the drivers of the D11's, we need practice time, and we need protection from you, so everyone, do your part and we might just scrape though this contract with limited casualties."

"Any other questions?"

Mr Yellow put his hand in the air, "I hear from other conversations boss, that we are paid by a third-party arrangement, is that true?"

"Oh, for fuck's sake, that's him stirring up the sediment in New York, he predicts that fear will keep them silent."

"So, we have whispering accounts to deal with who in the future could well speak when spoken too, correct sir?"

Mr Black started laughing again, "Ok, come on Mr Grey, just explain please!"

Mr Grey stood and stared at them, "Look, we just can't kill every fucker, come on, some are allowed to live, right, or what is this really then, just a tour for psychopaths?"

"We must educate and give them the fear factor, now this job will be the start, they will all look to who did this and the rumours are spreading already, I have intimated that it's another family from the other side of the river, and a few deaths in the city of English gangsters confirms the practice, that if they want to search and want to find us that they had better up their life insurance, get it?"

"Now, during a conversation with the New York Bankers, I expressed an idea for them, so, on seeing the death of these scum of the earth, that they could empty their bank accounts and run, get it, so they will be in the same boat as us, understand the concept gentlemen?"

Silence followed his speech for a few moments, but Mr Black broke the silence and gave them look, then answered their questions.

"Yes gentlemen, he is bonkers, and yes he's an evil genius, but he has our future in his head, so he is one of us, he just lacks the swimming practice and the survival instinct of the average orange, so I feel that we need to develop and train him up a little, yes?"

The placed erupted in laughter at Mr Black's comments.

As the laughter slowed down, a hand was raised for Mr Grey.

"Yes Mr Yellow?"

"Err Mr Grey, is it true that Jimmy the saw was chopped in New York City?"

He looked at Mr Black before attempting an answer, "I have to be honest with you, I wanted him in the mix to create that cloud of fear within their community, and him getting gunned down in the offices of our oh so honest lawyer firm, was poignant, because he was the ultimate scumbag, and I hear that his pet psychopaths bit the dust with him, it couldn't have happened to a uglier, nasty, dirty bunch of embarrassing humanity than them, and I thank the man who did the job, so, well done sir!"

"So, you knew the man then Mr Yellow?"

"A victim Mr Grey nothing more, so for my family I wish to thank Mr Black personally for our revenge!"

The room erupted again in shouting and clapping.

Mr Black had to stand and take the clapping, he held his hands up to stop them so he could explain, "Just this once, the alignment of work and bitter memory joined up and as Mr Grey had invited the man and his, for want of another word, his animals to the States, I knew that the execution had fallen to me and I shouldn't have, but I took great delight in killing them all, please excuse my long term grudge on a man who destroyed my life, but I suppose, brought me here in some way, he was the victim of time management, his time had run out!"

"Good riddance and I think he won't be missed."

The clapping started up again as they all stood to applaud him.

"And obviously your third party executed them then?" said Mr Black in Mr Greys ear over all the noise.

He nodded back to him, "All mixed bacon bits to the grill sir, so we will go with that explanation when we get the chance, eh?"

"And you will I suppose?"

"Oh, yes, we will get the chance to express our opinion, I'm thinking of investing in a newspaper, a good idea?"

"What the mornings edition or the complete company?"

"Both, are there any obvious choices out there, sir?"

Mr Black had to bend over, as he chocked and laughed at the mad man.

CHAPTER 25 ... ROADIES SLEEPING CABIN. CONSTRUCTION SITE.

The lads on the three story multi bunks snored as they slept, the grunts squeaks and farts, filled the air as Billy tried to sleep.

"So, labour day is celebrated on the first day of September, depending what day it falls on, so this year it will be Monday the 2nd, now that's good eh?"

No one answered his random statement, but the snoring had stopped.

"So, we have three days to practice, where do we order tarmac from again?"

"Shut.... up!" shouted Mr Black.

Everyone waited for what was to come because he was awake, and they all knew it.

"So, a very old grudge, right?"

"Yep!"

"Do you want to talk about it?"

"Nope!"

"Regrets?"

"Only that you won't shut up!"

"Retirement on Tuesday then?"

"Yep!"

"What should I do though?"

"Shut the fuck up!" shouted the whole cabin as one voice.

And hour later he was brought round by his phone buzzing, and he was physically thrown out of the sleeping cabin by a few of them.

Outside in the misty pre-dawn he finally answered the phone, "Yes!"

"Billy, what the hell's happening over there, the tv says that a bunch of English blokes have just been murdered in New York city, they were gunned down with a machine gun, so it's not you then?"

"Sandra, I'm speaking to you darling, yes?"

"Yes, sorry babe, I was just so worried, so who is it got killed?"

"Look, is Frank with you?"

"What in my bedroom at three in the morning, knob head?"

"Yes, sorry babe, look, the people who bit the dust were Jimmy the saw and his uglies, the lot bing, bang bosh, morgue bound, get it?"

"So, who killed him then?"

"Oh, you know what he was like, he obviously upset the yanks, touchy people you know Sand, especially when he goes around shouting at them, anyway, he won't be missed will he?"

"Well, no, he was a bloody animal!"

"Yes babe, agreed, look I was going to call you in the morning so I might as well say it now."

"To say what Billy?"

"Look, Sand, you have to go to the garage and kick Frank up the arse, he has to move and bloody quick, he's the new king of the west end club, he has to take control, understand?"

"But I can't tell him that, he won't listen to me Billy!"

"Sand, he's the only one who can bring the west end to some sort of order, he has to take the helm of a sinking ship, or the vacuum will be filled by morons, and we'll have a war on in London, get me babe?"

"Look, I'll tell him what you just said, but in can't insist Billy!"

"Oh yes you can, you are more of a gangster that all of them put together, just name your family members to them and see their eyes change with fear, besides that, Frank has contacts all over London, get him to make calls and take over, clear babe?"

"But why are we involved in all this Billy?"

"Babe, we are his family, he needs our support, and you need to give him a kick in the right direction for all of us."

"But if he doesn't want it, then what?"

"You'll find that he does want it, the fact is that an ugly was in his seat all along, you just see his face when you tell him, ok?"

"When?"

"This morning babe, the seat is still warm, and he has to go down east and make sure it's his, right?"

"Ok, I'll talk to Aunty Ivy when I get the chance."

"Who?"

"Aunty Ivy, his mother, the matriarch of the family, well, to smooth it all a little, yes."

"So, you were related to Jimmy?"

"No, just neighbours down east, my mams friend all along, we all were, Marge Cray was just down the road you know?"

"As in the Cray twins?"

"Yes, sister and another of my mams bingo buddies."

"I'm finding out more and more about my wife here Sand."

"Anyway, are you ok?"

"Yes babe, and you?"

"Oh, driving them around, I just drive, that's me!"

"And no guns?"

"They won't let me play with their kit babe, the amateur and all that, in fact, they've just thrown me out of the sleeping shed, they say I snore babe, that can't be right, can it?"

"Moron! You sleep like a pig, snorting and what not, but after all that I still miss you!"

"I miss you too Sand, look a week and I'll be back, ok?"

"So, the big one's coming up then?"

"Yes babe, so keep up with the news, try CNN or another American channels, apparently the Mafia have a war on."

"And that's good?"

"Well for us, yes, for them, very bad!"

"And you're in the middle of all this Billy?"

"No Sand, I'm in Florida, remember? Soaking up the sun and driving them around, that's it!"

"Just get it done and come home Billy."

"Sand, I've been thinking, perhaps we need to move?"

"Where too?"

"Switzerland perhaps?"

"Chocolate log land?"

"Yes, a nice mountain retreat, all the safety of seeing anyone who shows up, get it?"

"You're scaring me again Billy."

"Safer than London Babe, right?"

"Better air."

"And weather, snow in the winter, sun in the summer, we can learn to ski and walk the mountains, talk about keeping fit, that's us and our future, agreed?"

The phone was silent as she processed the decision through her brain, "Yes, agreed, I'll search for a nice place, how much do I spend?"

"You decide babe, just make it a place big, we never know who might pop round for a cup of tea, right?"

"Yes Billy, you never know, ok, I'll get onto it, good luck Billy Boncour, and do not get killed or I will kill you again, clear?"

"Clear sweetheart!"

He closed the call and suddenly missed home but realised that she was his home, and wherever she was he wanted to live and share his life with hers.

By the time he had finished the call it was fully light, and the sun was starting to burn off any lingering mist of the swamp on the horizon.

The rattle of an old engine struggling to get top revs entered the gate as a Dodge camper van came to a screeching stop in front of him and Mr Red wound the window down and grinned.

"Thanks for waiting up Mr Grey!"

He smiled at Mr Red, "Amazing you made it here with that water pump pully nearly falling off."

"Really, and that's what's wrong with the old girl?"

"That and the engine management system is not working correctly, because it should be able the rev higher than that."

"Oh, yes, a mechanic by trade, I remember now."

"And I see major problems with the old girl."

"Ah, so that's why all the lights are flashing on the dash then?"

"So, what trade did you do, back in the day?"

"A brick layer, back in the day, and Blue was a car salesman, but of the worst kind."

Billy now felt the tiredness creeping up on him, "Do you need to sleep lads, been driving all night I suppose?"

"Yes, perfect, so where to?"

Billy thumbed the sleeping hut behind him, "Ok, the deal is this, I fix your van, and I sleep in it, yes?"

"Well yes mate, this old junker is about done, so where do we go again?"

He thumbed to the sleeping container behind him as he watched Mr Blue struggle with his crutches and Mr Red helping him over to the sleeping container to crash out.

"A very grumpy bunch in there, lads, so I hope you don't snore, oh and welcome to Florida, and your friendly Highways repair hub, did you read the sign at the gate? No hard hats, no boots, no job!"

He opened the door, and they disappeared, but not before Mr Red gave him the middle finger to scratch his scalp as an insult for him to shut up and let them rest.

Billy patted the hood and whispered to the old van, "Don't you listen these nasty people, I'll sort you out darling, no probs!" He quickly climbed into their camper van, flopped onto the bed and was asleep in seconds.

Just four hours later he was woken again as someone banged on the side of the van and Mr Black voice echoes around the site, "Come on up you get, work to do, people to protect and a road to resurface!"

He couldn't believe his ears, "A road to resurface?"

Mr Black opened the door and shouted at him, "Come on, we're taking a look at the target, and a little run out for the monsters, yes?"

"The D11's?"

"Yes, we can get used to driving in a straight line and the turn into the lane for the big house, only this time we reverse out and come back, yes?"

"Err ... yes boss, keep em guessing right?"

"A practice for our timings as well, so up you get and let's go!" He tossed the hard hat with the high viz vest inside to him and walked away, "And put your bloody hat on!"

Half an hour later he climbed up to the cab and started the engine, he looked at the opposite machine and Mr Black was doing the same, he pulled his side window dawn, "And what is it we're doing?"

"Mr Black shouted back to him, "We're levelling the road to make it usable."

"But I thought you wanted it blocked?"

"Yes, on the day, but now we have to show that we are working to get the road done, so I follow you and try to make a job of it, shove all the old surface to the right of the road, we can make extra cover for our snipers."

"In broad daylight?"

"It's a road, just do it and shut up!"

Mr Grey followed his instructions and drove out of the gates behind the waist carrier truck.

He followed the truck down the road at his maximum speed of 20 mile per hour and carefully timed how long it took to reach the T junction for the hacienda, exactly an hour, he looked at the fuel level gauge and realised that he had just about run out of fuel.

Mr Black nodded to him, because he had come to the same conclusion, he stopped his D11, to talk to him, he slid the side window and shouted over, "We'll have to leave them here, and fuel them up here."

Mr Grey agreed with the idea as a police car came past them from another direction and stopped the surveyors van at the back of them, and talked to Mr Pink who was obviously talking to the officer in an American accent, the police car then drove off down the bumpy road.

Mr Blacks phone buzzed, "Yes Mr Pink, what's the problem?"

"A major problem sir!"

"Sir Mr Pink, what's up?"

"That cop has just made you sir and is about to call for confirmation from his station."

Mr Black blinked in shock, "How?"

"Apparently, they have pictures of us all sir, it's part of their works permissions process, checking on illegal workers from Mexico and all that, so what do we do?"

Mr Black stared at Mr Grey as he thought about it all, "Ok, all back to base and we conference the lads on this one!" he pointed to Mr Grey to jump down from the D11 and follow him to the surveyor's van.

Mr Grey followed in shock at his sudden movement, he looked at his watch as Mr Pink blew his whistle and shouted out.

"Ok, guys, we break for lunch, two hours and we'll be working late!"

Mr Grey looked on in confusion but climbed in the van to find out what was happening.

"Back to base now, everyone, we need a rethink and quick, ok, Mr Pink, go!"

"Why, what's up?"

"Mr Pink was an actor," said Mr Black.

"And that means what?"

"Look Mr Grey, we all have pictures on police walls as contractors for the roads, all part of enforcing regulated workers and not Mexican illegal's, standard practice, get it?"

"Shit!"

"Exactly, so now what do we do?"

Mr Grey touched Mr Pinks shoulder, "An actor, right?"

"Yes, RSC back in the day."

"So, you gave him the blab?"

"Yes, mid-western drawl yawl!"

"So, he knows you now, and you explained that you're the owner, right?"

Mr Black was sitting on the back seat and listening to the conversation.

"So, you have an opinion here Mr Grey?"

"Well, the pictures can't be us, can they, so they must be the others, the lads who were laid off because the company was going bust, yes?"

He turned to Mr Pink, "So what does he actually know about us?"

"Err, he's checking on the site, the situation with the road re-surface and the timing's, his boss was on the line busting his ass about it."

Mr Grey thumbed to the big house, "Because he had obviously complained, right?"

"Yes Mr Grey, we have to assume that, so now what?"

Mr Black scratched his beard and looked at the big house, "And if he's suspicious of the timing of us chipping up his road, then logically, he will have checked with the police, so he thinks he has our photos to check us out, so what's their next move Mr Pink?"

"He's reporting back and a big wig from city hall planners and will come and check the site and the work."

"But we have all the paperwork for doing this then?"

Mr Pink nodded to Mr Grey.

Mr Black turned on him and growled, "You do have public planning for what we're doing here, right?"

Mr Grey shook his head, "But hold up here, let me think!"

"So, we are trapped Mr Grey, do you understand that?"

Mr Grey's eyes moved from face to face as he thought about the problems.

"Bribery?" he asked optimistically.

Mr Black scowled at him in fumed silence.

Mr Grey gave Mr Pink a grin, "Ok, then, Mr Pink must ball's it out, quote his new title and how the company was bought out by a British company, and he was informed that this was his contract, to resurface this road, if, he's wrong then blame the British for sending him."

"And why would they send him her Mr Grey?" Mr Black scowled again.

"To fulfil contracts on the list, this was priority, obviously?"

"Very thin you moron!"

"And an excuse for a diversion."

"What?"

"We have to torch the police stationhouse, bad wiring in those old block houses."

"A complete washout, ok, we have to rethink and re-plan back at base." said Mr Black.

"Mr Brown used to be an electrician."

"Thanks Mr Pink." said Mr Grey.

"And a part time burglar as well." said Mr Black as his brain tried to work out a plan.

Mr Grey smiled at him again, before chirpily announcing a new plan, "Ah, so we burn the police station to the ground as a diversion to the main plan, but obviously we have to bring the plan forward, we can't give them time to investigate us, can we?"

Mr Black grabbed him by the collar, "Do you realise what you're asking to be done, you moron?"

"Well part of the initial plan, we would be better with a good diversion, just in case of a random cop car being nosey, and us having to kill an innocent?"

"Yes, agreed Mr Grey, we don't want to kill innocents, so how do we do this?"

"Ok, sir, give me five! So, In my mind I'm back to bribery again."

Mr Black stared down Mr Pink, "So when is he coming to inspect us and the gear?"

"Later today boss, but I suspect he has other motives, perhaps he's fishing for a bung?"

"You, see?" said Mr Grey.

Mr Black sniffed, "Ok, over to you Mr Pink, you are the mouth in all this, bribe if you can but give us time, clear?"

"Yes, clear boss!"

Mr Grey looked at him on the back seat, "We have no choice, we have to move now!"

"Over cooked Mr Grey, before we make the move, let us analyse our situation and new intelligence, so, Mr Pink, the cop identified me from what?"

"He showed me a picture from a passport photo and compared it to you in the D11."

Mr Grey's eyes locked onto Mr Black's, "Times up, right boss?"

Mr Black ignored him and tapped away at a text to all colours, Mr Grey looked over his shoulder at what he was writing, A GENERAL CONFERENCE IS CALLED, 13.00HRS.

He looked at Mr Pink then back to Mr Black for his final word.

"Ok, we might have to do this the old-fashioned way, attack at dawn and all that!"

Mr Grey could now see the panic in Mr Pink's eyes, but determination in Mr Black's.

He was silent as he and Mr Black were driven away, "What if they are following our phone convos?" he asked out loud.

Mr Black touched his shoulder, "Then we have to tighten our security even more, we turn to code, clear Mr Grey?"

"Yes sir, code!"

CHAPTER 26 ... ROADIES FOOD HUT ... CONSTRUCTION SITE.

Mr Black fiddled with his spaghetti, twisting and turning it before giving up and pushing the bowl away.

Mr Grey took it and smiled, "You don't want that, Mr Black?"

Mr Black stared through him as he thought about the new problem in their midst.

Mr Grey continued to eat as he looked around the faces

"Ok," said Mr Black, "The whisper has obviously gone around so let's have some intel, Mr Green on our security?"

Mr Green also didn't touch his spag boll, "Sir, we have to assume that they know all about us and why we are here."

"Why?"

"Well, they have a photo of you, and that means that they know you from past contracts."

"Why and how would that be?"

"We must assume that they have feelers everywhere, including the police, all parts of business and social contacts, possibly even border controls, that's where the photo must have come from."

Mr Black fell silent then searched the faces for answers, "Ok, Mr Brown, what have you got to say?"

"Sir, in my opinion they don't have a clue, I talked to the gate guards, and they are looking forward to the party on Monday, a big shindig by all accounts, perhaps they have intel on us, but not much."

"Given anything away Mr Brown?"

"Only what you wanted spreading sir, the takeover of the road construction company and Mr Pink being the multi-millionaire who spreads it about to friends, yes?"

"Good, so this could be a come on from one of them wanting a bung, yes?"

"Feelers perhaps, but they don't know us, I'm convinced of that."

"Ok, now Mr Pink, what have you achieved from talking to the cop?"

"Err ... we have the cops on our side sir, they want the road done and dusted and quick, I gave the cop a good drink to initiate any questions asked about us from any direction, and he agreed to help our cause, with a promise of more funds for his family vacation."

"And you said what?"

"Well I gave him a grand in cash and he was happy to help, then I said that some of our workers are from out of town, he understood the meaning of that, but mentioned his bosses wanting to show willing for the local politicians by finding none union and none native workers here in Florida working illegally, he understood the meaning, and I simply said that for the work to get done quickly he had better hold off the morons and leave us alone, he seemed to be switched on to the politico's involved here sir."

"So, if not, we would stop working, right?"

"Yes sir, and they would have the unions on their backs!"

"And embarrass town hall, yes?"

"Yes sir, leave us alone or face disruption of your whole road network, I pointed to the D11's and how much muck they can move in one go!"

"Good, anything else gentlemen?" he searched the faces and stopped at Mr Blue, "Come on then Mr Blue out with it please?"

"Sir, why are we doing this, why wait, why not go now and get it done, forget party's and people coming and going, just roll up and fulfil the contract?"

"Anyone else?" he looked at Mr Red who nodded to him, "And Mr Red's view?"

"I agree with Blue, why wait, it's just wasting time and our security will only get compromised by just the normal bods, the cop, the cabbie, or simply a lost dog, whatever, the more time we piss about, the more chance of being disrupted or found out by those people at the big house, they are not idiots, they see the signs of movement and I imagine that some of them are worried about road works, it all smacks of a plan by someone out there sir!"

Mr Black turned to Mr Grey, "And the spag eater?"

"Well, as I see it sir, we are ready, the party frocks for the D11's perhaps, but an overall plan for the attack and we go, the timing however is for you to decide sir, so over to you."

"And afterwards gentlemen?" he searched their faces for an answer, "Look, if we have tags then our extraction could become very complicated, so I feel that we need more information, on all this, so Mr Pink, I'd like you to follow up the police, find his links and confirm or deny what they have on us, clear?"

"Clear sir."

"And take Mr Green with you for your personal security, call him your chauffer or something."

Mr Pink nodded.

"And don't let him speak, they'll spot his Scottish accent a mile away!"

"Sir!"

"Ok, my conclusion and you can all throw in any alternate action, but I think we should stay on schedule, because it is out best shot to keep them all together, so, for me we stick to the planned Monday night Tuesday morning for the action, any objections?"

The faces stared back at him in silence.

"Ok, unanimous decision, ok?"

"But it's a what we would call a bank holiday," said Mr Grey, "The whole weekend will be slow, it's party time for all workers, maybe we should do the same?"

Mr Black pointed to him, "Yes, a good point, ok, we have a break and prepare for the end of the weekend."

"Ok, Mr Brown will conduct visitors to the house down the rough road, he will be our ears and eyes until Monday evening and their big bash, Mr Purple will block the western end of the road and report anything unusual, anyone really curious, clear all?"

"What about the D11's boss?" asked Mr Grey.

"Ok, fuel them up and leave them there till we need them, you Mr Grey, are a mechanic, take Mr Yellow and work on the D11's, but pay attention to the neighbour's, clear?"

"Right, it's now Friday afternoon, today is a clean-up day, tomorrow we go about normal routines, show a bit of willing with the road but no contact with the big house or any of their people."

"What about the armour for the D1's sir?" asked Mr Grey.

"On site when we're ready, are the ready to be fitted Mr Purple?" said Mr Black.

"Yes sir, just clip on and a few modifications to the bucket."

"Such as?"

"Well, you'll need a bit of weight in the buckets, or you'll roll all over the place, plus the momentum of a heavier vehicle can help sir."

"Yes agreed, ok, slack time, clean and prep please."

"But we have to finish the road sir!" said Mr Grey.

Mr Black looked around again, "Well does anyone know how to do this job then?"

The laughing started and Mr Yellow pointed to Mr Orange.

Mr Black laughed with them and nodded to Mr Orange, "Ah, the boy from the black stuff, I knew you would come in handy one day, so you have experience of road building then?"

"A civil engineer sir, well before I got into trouble, I didn't mean to......"

"Stop, we do not swop reasons for being here, we do not tell back stories, we are all silent about our past, me included, so you can organise all this?"

"Er ... yes sir but we need outside contractors to help us."

Mr Black glared at him to finish his statement and quick.

"Oh, er ......truckers to take away the spoils, tarmac delivery scheduling, with a none stop hot service and of course a Bloornox hot leveller and layer, with a cooling sprayer on the back, oh, and a road roller to finish off, then lines men, to repaint the road lines, then a final inspection from the county to sign off the contract, or we won't get paid, sir!"

The laughing started up again as none of them understood what he needed.

"Well, we're not employing anyone else so improvise please Mr Orange."

"But we've vandalised a State highway sir, there will be repercussions."

Mr Black turned to Mr Grey and scowled again, "You see how your simple plan can get very complicated? Your idea is getting out of hand Mr Grey!"

Mr Grey looked at the faces laughing at him as he thought through the new problem, then smiled as it came to him.

"Well, we know where we can dump the spoils, and we have the D11's to flatten out the road for the tarmac contactors to do their stuff, we simply hand over to them to finish off, after all we've done all the work, right?"

"Will someone please translate what the moron is on about."

Mr Grey continued as the laughing faded, "The target area, when we've finished sir, will be a hollow in the ground and a hollow in the ground needs levelling off with our road spoil, bing, bang, bosh!"

"So, we bury them under the spoil from the road Mr Grey?" asked Mr Black.

"Just an hour's, work after the contract is fulfilled, then we split and ka-ching all round!"

The room erupted in laughing again at the simple answer.

"Well, there we have it kids, from the lips of the genius, we bury the victims, now that's going to be a new one for those looking for bodies, right?"

"As a sign of our complete contempt for them sir!" said Mr Pink.

Mr Black pointed to him and smiled, "Yes boy, a sign of our contempt for these people who sell misery and death all over the world, yes good!"

"So, anything else to discuss, while we're all together?"

"Sir!" said Mr Pink, "Myself and Mr Green will need to visit a bar where the police drink sir?"

"And you want permission to start drinking?"

"Contract rules could be put aside sir for this one-off engagement, perhaps?"

Mr Black focused on Mr Green and stared, "Yes, wine, but if I smell whiskey on you Mr Green, I will............"

"Beat the crap out of you!" echoed the room as the laughing started up again.

"Do not let that crazy bastard drink whiskey, he's allergic to alcohol, and he's a berserker if he starts, his only talent, understand Mr Pink, nothing, besides, he's driving right, so juice for him, yes?"

CHAPTER 27 ... CHUNKY MONKEYS ... BAR AND GRILL.

Mr Pink entered the bar at the western swing doors and all faces turned to him, Mr Green followed on and whispered in his ear, "Cowboys, the lot of em, Pinky!"

"Yee, hah!" screeched Mr Pink.

That set off the laughing from the bar and everyone seemed to relax as the strangers walked in and sat down on the high stools at the bar.

A cop moved over to them and handed Mr Pink a glass, "On me buddy, local brew, cool with you guys?"

"Err .... No, wine for me Jonney."

The cop was going to drink it himself, but Mr Green took it instead, "Thanks mate, very nice of yee!"

He looked to Mr Pink for an explanation.

"He's Scotch, and they say up there do not give the animals anything to drink, get me Jonney?"

The cop turned to Mr Green and was handed the glass back, "Very nice, anything stronger?"

The cop turned to Mr Pink again for another explanation of the space alien.

"Give my chauffeur drink and he will wreck this place Jonney, nil by mouth please!"

Jonney's face changed as he started laughing, "You're crazy Mr Pinkerton!"

"No Jonney, he is." He thumbed to Mr Green who was looking round at people looking at him.

"Hey. Pinks, they have an arm-wrestling machine, come on matey, let's do this!"

Jonney and his friends watched the mad Scot take on the albatross arm wrestling machine as the laughing started up again.

Within ten minutes people were placing bets on how many levels he could take; then someone bought him a long drink of something that looked like bourbon with ice.

"Nil by mouth for him please!" he shouted to them, but he was ignored as Green took it to another level of power on the machine, someone slotted in the coins for him to give it another try."

The chants of the bar started off, "Jock, Jock, Jock, Jock, Jock!"

Mr Pink tried to ignore the mayhem Mr Green was now causing in the slot machines area.

He turned to Jonney, "You see what I'm up against here Jonney, bonkers, the lot of them, do you see my problem letting them loose on the American public?"

"Keep him on the chain gang, huh?"

He pointed, exactly, "So who's the guy in the photo of you showed me earlier?"

Jonney took out the photo from his top pocket and handed it to him, "An all points notice of a man of international interest."

"By whom?"

"The FBI want this guy for murdering English guys in New York City, a blood bath apparently."

"And you've seen him?"

"Well, I thought he looked like the guy driving your big hitter."

"The D11, wow, he gets about then, Tommy's been with the company for months, I always wondered what the guy gets up to on their vacations."

Jonney burst into laughter again.

"Yeah, sorry Pinkerton, say, are you related to the company, you know, Pinkertons investigation agency, the, we always get our man people?"

He gave him a wide toothy grin, "Na, I'm the black sheep of the family, I went to college, and I became a civil engineer, far too correct for some of the family, boring man!"

"Really, so the money came from them then?"

"Hey, don't start on me just because my great grand pop, made a living with the FBI, and got shot while working on a case."

"Did he?"

"Yeah, prohibition, he was in the middle of all that shit!"

"Bad?"

"Oh, nasty man, well, the New York police, NYPD, Irish you see, they didn't see the point, so he had to fight for the law."

"Yeah, I get you buddy, some of us have to really fight to maintain the real law."

"So how does this all points things work then?"

"Well, it's you who should be telling me man, being related to the guy who invented all this."

"A civil engineer, remember?"

"Well, just a man of interest, some guy has a photo of a man who's done something really bad, and it gets printed out, country wide, if your D11 driver Tommy was this dude then I ring it in and they arrive, get it?"

"Hey, an easy way of getting rid of my D11 driver if he causes me problems, eh?"

"You bettya buddy, his feet wouldn't touch the State line, helicopter and gone baby!"

"I have a helicopter, but hey, I ain't bringing it here for these ass hole to scratch with a truck or something!"

"Really, so you fly it?"

"Na, the moron does that!"

"The Jock?"

"Yeah, not as stupid as he looks, British army trained, hey, he might be on that all points thing then?"

"For what?"

Mr Pink pointed to Mr Green who was in the process of breaking the machine.

"See what I mean?"

Jonney burst into laughter again, "Are all your guys like him?"

"Yep, afraid so, all fruit cakes, mixed with too many nuts!"

Mr Green had collapsed on the floor in exhaustion as the crowd were screaming in laughter, the machine was now on its side and coins were dropping out making a clonking noise.

"You, Yanks, can't even make a slot machines! This bloody thing is crap!"

Mr Pink shouted over the top of the mayhem, "You, my so-called chauffeur, get in the God dammed car and I'll drive the thing this time, and by the way, you're fired!"

"No, don't be like that Pinkerton, give the guy a break, he's just having fun man!"

Mr Pink looked at the faces, "He's just saved your job, ass wipe!"

Mr Green fell over again and burped.

What the hell has he been drinking?"

One of them nodded to the empty glasses on the little table.

"Bourbon with ice!"

"How many?"

"Err .... Ten maybe?"

"He's my driver you guys!"

The laughing started up again as he pointed to Mr Green, "Ok, slam him in my car, I'll drive, the drunken bum!"

Mr Pink shook hands with Jonney, "Keep in touch, we could use a cop on our side now and again.

Jonney pointed to the drunk, "Yeah, I can see why!"

Going down the freeway, Mr Green sat up in the back seat, "So, did you get what we wanted?"

Mr Pink smiled in the driver's mirror, "Yes, and our Mr Black is wanted country wide for the New York Killings, an all-points bulletin in all police stations, so now what do we do?"

"Shit!"

"Anyway, aren't you pissed as a fart?"

"What, drinking that cat piss, do me a favour! Besides, it was business, right?"

"Yes Green, it was business, but now what is he going to do, it was him then?"

Me Pink stared at him, "And you, shut the fuck up!"

"Yes, sorry, that's a very bad contract ......"

"Policy!" said Mr Pink finishing on of the old man's mantras, "We all shut the fuck up, clear?"

Mr Green nodded but burped, "Sorry!"

"So, I wonder if the target has that news with his morning breakfast?"

Me Green was gone and sleeping again.

"We'll have to do this without the old man Mr Green!"

"Well, you can give him the good news Pinky, because I'm not!"

"But he's under threat?"

"Now that will just get him motivated and that means get out of his way, clear so far Mr Pinkerton?"

"He's bad in a full contact then?"

"Hey, the Vikings call them berserker's and he is, so do not rouse him in public, understand?"

"Wow, I didn't realise."

"Not been on a contract before the Pinks?"

"No, just security and research."

"Well, this is where the machine touches the road, we are the tread on those tires."

"Burning rubber?"

"Oh, yes, burning everything including rubber, did you hear about his New York trip?"

"Shut up, you know the contract rules, we shut the fuck up!"

"Yeah, sorry Pinky!"

CHAPTER 28 ... ST MARTIN IN THE FIELDS CHURCH ... LONDON.

Sandra looked for the white-haired elderly woman dressed in black on the front seats during the memorial service, she listened to the hymn sung by the magnificent choir, tears dripped down her face as she watched the woman cry and felt her pain at losing her last surviving son.

When the bishop had finished his closing prayers and silence descended the woman stood and looked around to see who had come to the service.

She locked eyes with Sandra and saw the tear streeks down her cheek, she smiled over to her and shook hands with some but made her way over to her.

"Freddy Binton's girl, I knew you'd be here darling, only we women remember the scum bags, don't we darling? Only us to do the crying right?"

"Right aunty Ivy, I know that my mam would have been here if she were alive, no one else cares do they aunty?"

Ivy gave her a great big hug and a kiss, then stood away and looked at her, "Family ok darling?"

"Billy is a pain in the arse as usual but apart from that, good, all doing good, sorry to hear about Jimmy, was it sudden?"

Ivy smiled at her and dragged her out of the chapel and into the sunlight, "Gunned down in broad daylight in New York, he was playing in the big league and didn't realise the rules, like a lamb to the slaughter and his mates, splat, the lot of em!"

"Oh, dear aunty Ivy, so who did it?"

"Yanks, some Don over there didn't like my Jimmy, well who did, eh darling?"

"Yeah aunty, who did?"

"What a mess, now what do I do? Sorry darling I forgot your name, what was it again?"

Sandra smiled and took her arm as they walked, "Well, I'm married now, so my name is Sandra Boncour, yeah, I know but that's his stupid name!"

The old lady hugged her again, "Now don't you worry about a name, so is he useful darling?"

"Oh, very, he's in Florida at the moment, working."

"In the game?"

"Afraid so aunty."

"Dangerous you know darling; he might not come home you know?"

"I'll kill him if he doesn't aunty, the little toe rag!"

Ivy laughed with her, "It's good to talk to a girl from the east end sweetheart, did you hear about the Turks trying it on down west?"

"In what way?"

"Muscling in with the clubland, trying to buy the whole damn lot, no chance obviously!"

"I have a sponsor if you need one aunty, Billy's old boss up north, one of Jimmy's old pals in fact."

"A good pal?"

"Very close at one time, should I give him the word?"

The old woman looked at the beautiful church and started to cry again, "Ugly old world, don't you think Sandra?"

"Yes aunty, very ugly sometimes, and this could get worse, don't you think?"

"What, if we don't get a sponsor in the big seat and bloody quick?"

"Exactly aunty, "Frank Warren, do you know him?"

"Na, do I need to?"

"Well, not really aunty, I'll give him a bell and get the seat filled, yes?"

"And if I don't?"

"Well, the piss pot pension won't last will it, so the club will go down the drain for a start and also you might have people wanting to take the piss aunty?"

"They wouldn't dare!"

"Ugly new world aunty, best get yourself protected and bloody quick!"

"And this bloke will do that?"

"He'll keep order aunty, look, you know how it goes, some tosser will try it on, and that will be the civil disturbance ending in deaths, all very nasty, you know that don't you, aunty?"

Ivy wiped her face with the black veil and stared at her, "Yes, tell him to take the seat and he's blessed by me, ok with all that?"

"I'll tell him aunty Ivy, leave it with me darling!"

"Those animals need discipline; and can he provide that?"

"They had better not try it on with him aunty, very nasty when roused, get me?"

"Good, give him my regards please, and tell him to get it sorted, your family I suppose?"

"Yes aunty, my family, he'll do the job, no probs, yes?"

She stopped and gave Sandra another hug and a kiss, "Bastard men, bloody useless without our leadership don't you think darling?"

"Oh, absolutely aunty, without a kick up the arse now and again where would we all be, right?"

Ivy burst out laughing at Sandra and her old-fashioned views on men she agreed with.

Sandra escorted her to the limo parked at the side of the road and watched the chauffeur open the back door for the fragile old lady in black and held her hand to help her in to sit down.

Ivy buzzed the window down to speak to here, "And my pension?"

"Plus, expenses aunty, Frank will be there for you whatever, ok with that?"

"Yes babe, ok with all that, get him to pop in for a cuppa, can you?"

"Will do darling, leave it with me for now, I'll ring you later. ok?"

The old lady buzzed the window back up and started to cry again, Sandra waved her off into the traffic, then punched in the number on her phone.

"Frank, yes, I've talked to her, and she sends her love, so get moving please!"

"But Sandra, is this right?"

"Frank, just move your arse and get over there, you are the big seat, get it?"

"That's what Billy said to do, but I have no bods with me!"

"Take the farts and play the game, the new broom and all that, look, if you don't, others will, understand?"

"But I don't own the club?"

"Yes, you do, me and Billy have just bought 29% and aunty Ivy has the 51%, and you now have 10% of the clubland PLC."

"What, floated on the stock exchange?"

"Yes, those bank farts do come in handy sometimes Frank!"

"Casinos, dance and leisure facilities?"

"Yep, the lot, and it's about time you had a proper job, Uncle Frank."

"Am I?"

"Yes, you are, me and Billy are your family, remember?"

"Am I?"

"You said it yourself back in the office, remember, so do it and prove my Billy right."

"Why, what did he say?" but the phone was now dead in his ear.

CHAPTER 29 ... SITE OFFICE ... ROADWAYS ... FLORIDA.

Mr Black listened to the conversation on the phone, he closely watched Mr Pink talking down the line and Mr Grey whispering to him now and again words of advice and encouragement.

"Look buddy, I'm under pressure from the county and I'm the owner of this new company so this is my chance to make a name, get me guy, I need this, so labour day, got people to work on labour day?"

He held the phone away from his ear as the swearing started up down the line.

"Ok, ok buddy, keep the pants on! So, the day after then? Ok, and I'm paying big bucks for this favour, understood, way over the rates, so give me a price?"

He held phone in the air again as Mr Grey listened and nodded to the price.

"Ok, so just to clarify for my boys, so this is going to be a hot continuous lay, no blips and bumps, then lined out the day after, correct?"

Mr Black stared at Mr Grey for an answer to the unasked question and Mr Grey gave him the sign language for the road surface and the new tarmac lay.

"Oh." grinned Mr Black.

Mr Grey also made the sign to Mr Pink who was still conversing down the line.

"Now listen up, the main highway will be closed at both ends, so you can rock and roll, clear, oh, and we planned a new heliport for the new breed of yuppy guys, get me?"

"Yeah, yeah, extras and more extras, we can pay for any extras, no prob's baby!"

He listened to the phone conversation in silence for a while then smiled at Mr Grey.

"Direct transfer on completion, no messing full payment up front the day after it's done, good for you buddy?"

"Ok, so from us you will have a flat road, fully hard cored ready to roll and an acre of land the cover, same again, it'll be flat and ready, clear so far, edges as you like we ain't fussy, just don't embarrass me with the county planners, understood?"

"Ok, bud, I'm cool with all that, so let me hand you over to my accountant to take the numbers for the bank transfer and I hope we can do business in the future, ok, I'm putting you through now, hold the line please.

He handed Mr Grey the line and smiled.

"Hello, Zebra, accounts!"

Mr Grey winked to Mr Black who was starting to enjoy the bad acting.

"Oh, yes, Mr Pinkerton has recommended you lot to do the job, ok, so I need numbers, because it will be a direct transfer from London, hey parent company and all, that, so, I know but this is the big old world mate, so pull up the pants and get the job done, the payment is scheduled for the day after, correct?"

He wrote the bank numbers down as the man spoke down the line.

"Ok, thank you for that and we hope to work with you in the future, yes, English owners, yes mate, all posh and transferred from the city of London."

"Ok, just to warn you, our home office will contact you to confirm what we have agreed on, clear, then she will check you out for reliability and future works in the pipeline, yes, a pipeline, didn't Mr Pinkerton tell you sir? We have other contract on the books, he's slightly stressed by it all, ok, we'll see you on Tuesday morning then, bright and early please, he's a bit of a stickler for punctuality, thank you sir and good day!"

Mr Black was bursting to ask the question but didn't want to sound too eager, so he grinned.

"And?"

Mr Pink side glanced Mr Grey before answering him.

"Ok, we will have an unfinished road surface and a great big lump on the horizon so Mr Grey thought of making a heliport, well it'll be big enough and the ground will be ready, right?"

Mr Black had to laugh at the stupid new plan, "So, they'll be dead buried and then tarmacked over, am I right here gentlemen?"

They both nodded to him, before he burst out laughing again, "Bonkers, the pair of you!"

"But we need a happy ending boss!" said Mr Grey.

"And we will have time for all this?"

"A clear extraction you said, no tails or follow on's you said?"

"But we can't just do this, what about the county planning?"

"Oh, our planner is dyslexic, and he read the plans wrong and gave us this site, sorry everyone! We'll do better next time," said Mr Pink.

Mr Black couldn't stop laughing at the stupid idea, "Better get to work then, let's get moving with the road hard core, do we have a road roller?"

Mr Grey grinned, "Working on Sunday boss, too obvious for witnesses?"

"No, all quite normal for people on time bonuses, best spread the news to the lads, clear?"

"Clear boss!"

Two hour later they were all working on the road and some bad acting continued as some of the lads took an unofficial break and Mr Pink gave them a public telling off.

Mr Black looked on as he laughed at the pantomime continuing down road they had already destroyed.

Mr Yellow walked by carrying a temporary road sign and Mr Green and Mr Orange carried the temporary traffic lights to control traffic.

Mr Black looked round form the cab of his D11 and locked eyes with Mr Grey as he looked at them below them, his comic grin brock Mr Black into uncontrollable laughter.

The arrival of a highways county planning department car stopped all thoughts stopped as panic took over that their plan might all fall apart, Mr Pink stepped out of his van to greet the county officials with a big smile.

Mr Black looked on as the map was pulled out of a brief case and spread over the hood of their car and watched Mr Pink waffled on and on trying to define what they wanted him to do, he shrugged his shoulders many times and shook his head as he tried to talk his way out of it all, eventually he stood firm and shouted out to the lads.

"Ok, we are out of here, they can do this themselves, shut it all down Rudy!"

Mr Black watched their faces as Mr Pink was now boiling up into an argument with county officials and now shutting it all down.

"You can't do this you moron," he mumbled.

But was then to his surprise, the officials backed down and pointed to the road to finish but Mr Pink hadn't finished his criticism of the county planning office and how he and his men were working overtime to finish the job they had sanctioned, he waved the commissioning certificate at them in frustration and the fact that he was paying double time for all this.

Mr Black, from his vantage point giggled at Mr Pinks, fumed and blustered, he gave him a silent hand clap for his complete confusion argument.

He then burst into laughter again as he saw Mr Pink's dyslexia diagnosis came into play; the officials didn't know what to say in return.

A senior planner pointed to the road and to get it finished as soon as possible, Mr Pink pulled out his phone and handed it to the official, he had obviously passed over the tarmac laying contractors to the man and looked on as the arguments continued.

Eventually they gave up stormed off and climbed back into their car, then drove off.

Mr Black and Mr Grey who could see it all gave him a round of applause as he took a bow.

"Flash bugger Mr Pink!"

Mr Pink winked then walked off shouting at the crew to get working again.

Mr Pink pointed to the spoil heaps to be shifted to the side of the road and to move it, and then shouted for Mr Grey to start his levelling runs on the road.

CHAPTER 30 ... HIGHWAY MAINTANANCE CREW ... FLORIDA STATE.

The two D11 bulldozers were levelling the road surface and leaving giant piles of the old road surface to one side to be used the next day, some of the lad's used shovels and picks to clear debris and other obstructions.

Mr Black slid back his window in the D11 and shouted out to Mr Yellow, "About time you lot were put in the chain gang, well overdue in my mind!"

He received a middle finger sign as Mr Yellow scratched his head under the hard hat, but despite the unhelpful criticism he carried on grafting.

Suddenly a limousine pulled up on the rough roads and started handing out cans of beer to the workers, Mr Green thanked the American for his thoughts, but Mr Black noted from his high position in the D11 cab, that the man noted Mr Greens Scottish accent and again worried it would all fall apart.

"Hey, all you guys are invited to the hacienda for the shindig, we all have fun and down a few beers, ok guys?" shouted the driver of the limo.

Mr Pink stopped in his works van and walked over to the limo, "Say, wow, thanks for that guy, wonderful to be appreciated for the work, but we're all on time penalties, we should have finished a week ago, so we have to rock and roll, ok guy?"

The man smiled at him and shook his hand, "Just a thanks for repairing our road, but what was wrong with it in the first place?"

"Oh, breaking up into sections, it would have disintegrated without this refresh, we might even be working tomorrow just to get it done, sorry guy, give your boss our apologies please."

"No, you can't work on a labour day, just relax people, it'll get done in the end, we aren't worried!"

"You ought to be." Mumbled Mr Black as he listened to the conversation.

"So, is that guy Scotch?"

"Oh, don't start him off guy, you know how these people can get with an insult?"

The man stared laughing, "I insulted him, how'd I do that?"

"Scotch is drink man and Scotland is his country, get it?"

"Ah, so are they all foreigners here?"

"No, just us man, damned white trash, the lot of us, eh?"

"So, are you Italian then?"

"Na, Irish German, Mexican, you?"

"Polish Italian."

Mongrels the lot of us, right?"

"We sure are buddy, we sure are!" he burst into laughter then got in his car and drove off back to the hacienda.

Mr Black watched him drive off up the lane and worried again that they were in some part busted, he moved the Heckler closer to his foot on the floor, just in case the action started.

He looked over to Mr Grey who was levelling off a section of road and nodded down the lane, but Mr Grey was too absorbed with the work.

"Good boy Mr Pink and earning your corn today I see, "Mumbled Mr Black.

Mr Grey signalled to him that he was almost out of fuel, so Mr Black gave Mr Pink the sign for the shutdown for the day.

On the way back to camp in the company minibus Mr Grey had an opinion, "I think we've been observed, and we've been twigged, so we have to go in the morning, agreed Mr Black?"

Mr Black turned to Mr Green for his opinion on the matter.

"Err ... I agree with him sir, lots of questions from the gate guards about our multi-cultural workers and not many Hispanics on the pay roll, we're either white trash red necks or we're the FED's, I see the looks here boss!"

Mr Black investigated the faces as he worked it out, "So, if they think we're the FED's then they'll be wondering why here, and why now, any other opinions here?"

Mr Brown coughed, and the faces turned to him to listen, "We have to move now, this is getting serious, these people are not idiots, the county planners were obviously sent to sort this out, and will have reported it all back I think, they will be doing research on faces, so how long can we mess about doing this business, we have to move and now!"

"Either way, we are giving them time to arm up aren't we Mr Brown?"

"Exactly sir, we don't have a real option here."

"Ok, agreed, so a finally planning meeting tonight!"

CHAPTER 31 ... FOOD HUT ... WORKS COMPOUND ... FLORIDA.

Mr Black scraped his plate and nodded his complements to Mr Pink the chef who had produced a fine meal, the chant started up as he laughed with them

"Plan, plan, plan, plan, plan, plan!"

He waved them down to stop then gave them the glare to listen and shut up.

"Well, this is the most ridiculous contract I have ever been involved it, completely bonkers on all fronts, but I don't see another way, so we are on a go situation, the obvious thing here is the timing, they won't expect an attack on labour day and certainly not in the early hours, and as an extra bonus, when this is all over we'll have a clean-up and prep time down so, any comments before I start the brief?"

The hut burst out laughing at his statement before he waved them to silence again.

"Well, I obviously need to retire from this mad, and bad world with a new planner in our midst who is not a colour, but we have to listen to talent, and he has that in spades, so we listen to his overall plan then I will take on the details, so, Mr Grey the overall plan please!"

They applauded him as he stood up to speak. "Err ... we roll up and kill them all by running them over and crushing the whole edifice of buildings into the environment, as the Romans would say, not one stone set upon another, total desolation, no evidence that they were ever here, understood?"

The rumbles of laughter slowed to a stop as he stared at them, "For our future safety this has to be done, everyone in that compound is going to be killed, no mercy given or received by these people, Mr Black reminded me the other day how it all works, as you all know, I'm new to all this, but as you also know, I'm quick at learning, so, to get at me and you, they would have tortured and killed our loved ones to gain information on us, bare that in mind as both you and I exterminate these maggots of our society, they bring misery and death to millions, and we are doing what Nations can't, we are the extermination crew, so death to them all, clear!"

The whoops and whistles subsided as Mr Black stood to speak. "Now listen up arse holes, this is the contract, we kill them all, no survivors will be taken, so, item one, is death to them all, and item two is this, anyone of us who gets himself killed will be taken away and buried properly by us, these are our dead, and we will do right by our Brethren, clear?"

"Clear!" shouts echoed through the food hut.

He waved them down again to silence, "Ok, at," he looked at his watch then back to their faces.

"At 23.00 tonight the road will be blocked both ends, no flow through, turn vehicles around if needed, Mr Brown and Mr Green will see to that and keep in contact with me for any changes to the target site, clear?"

Mumbles and coughs followed as he stared them down.

"So, at 24.00 the D11's will be refuelled, the armour party frocks fitted along with any weaponry needed at 02.00, the place will be lit up with perimeter lighting and people will be awake and possibly watching, so we need to be aware!"

"At 02.45, sniper pits will be dug and positions taken up for the shooting, all corners of the compass please, but none on or near the roadway!"

"At 03.00 we are on the move, so as we warm up the engines the noise might wake some of them to take up defensive positions, let's hope they are not military trained, just the usual thugs and scum bags from the city."

"So, 0310 we hit them and hard, periwinkle and I will do the work, all you lot have to do is kill all stragglers or people wanting to have a go and if needed take out people taking shots at the D11's."

"All runners and stragglers will be killed on site, gate guards first please, the obvious roundup point for the enemy to make a stand."

"Mr Red is with me in the rear bucket and Mr Blue is with Mr Grey in the same position, cannons fully loaded and ready to fire by 02.00."

"The roll up has to be a surprise to them, so not too much movement on the roads please, anyone on the road at this time will be killed because they will be the enemy!"

"Sniper over cover should be a covert approach and dig, not seen until the shooting starts, and give the D11's space if we get too close, remember that we can't see you in a fox hole so think clearly where you dig your cover hole, I don't want to kill morons who haven't thought about their positions, clear, so, any questions before we have desert, what is for desert by the way, Mr Pink?"

"Err .... Eaton mess sir!"

"Crushed meringue and strawberries with mixed cream, clever Mr Pink, the irony is noted."

"So, any other questions?"

The room was silent as the desert was served out to them one by one and all waited for Mr Black to receive his before they started.

"And remember this, to live the life and you have the skills to survive, you can ....?"

"Live the life and strive!" shouted the colour man before starting to eat.

It seemed like a blessing from the man who had trained these killers to within an inch of their lives and expected results from the next morning's work.

Mr Black winked at Mr Grey, and for the first time mixing with these people he felt at home.

The old man waved the spoon in the air to get them focused again, "Now if any of you leave prints, DNA or any evidence of occupation here before we leave, then I hope they fry you, because you will be a moron! We leave nothing to find, clear?"

"Clear!" echoed around the room as he looked at the faces, he always looked at their faces before any action and worried again for any loss they might incur.

"This had better work you bloody head case!" he shouted over to Mr Grey.

He received Mr Greys best toothy grin in return.

CHAPTER 32 ... ROADWORKS ... HIGHWAY YARD.

In the late evening Mr Black, started his exercises on the pull up bars erected by the others for their own work outs, with each pull up he asked a question to Mr Grey.

"What in hells name made you buy a bloody road construction company, you moron?"

"A hook sir, for on commers, a just in case, some future over cover."

Mr Black held the hight on the bar as he looked at him, "An over plan?"

"Yes Mr Black, just in case we have researchers wanting to find out some details."

He did another couple of pull ups as he grunted then stopped in the high position again and held it there as he asked.

"Do you not realise what will come for us if this fails sonny?"

"Yes sir, the world and an army."

"Sure, eh?"

"Just in case sir, and if they do pick up this trail then we have to come up with another plan."

Mr Black did another ten pull ups then dropped down to talk, "You have no idea sonny."

Mr Grey sniffed, "Well my granddad was in the army in world war 2, and he had ideas on this sort of thing, for instance, he used to say that it was very bad policy to follow the enemy if he was on the run through the jungle, always best get ahead and set a kill zone then wipe them out all in one go!"

"So, this is your granddads idea then?"

"No, mine, just a little change here and there."

Mr Black sniffed the started his stretching exercises and he asked again, "So what regiment was he in then?"

"The Green Howards, and Burma with the Chindits, he was full of all this hard-earned wisdom and no one to pass it onto."

"Except you, eh?"

"Yes sir, except me."

"And how did he end up?"

"Cashiered, ten bob in his pocket a suit, with a kick up the arse and to never show his face to them ever again."

"A bad boy then?"

"Oh yes, and he would have been very useful to your boys sir, oh yes, the old man had a vast experience of killing, so much so that it embarrassed them in the war office, show some mercy they said to him, eat shit he told them, and then told them how his friends were killed by the Japs, mercy my arse he would say, he was on an extermination plan from day one sir."

"I miss the old man myself Mr Grey."

"Yes sir, so do I, hence the prep for any followers, investigators or even the FBI, CIA, one never knows eh?"

"For those who follow your tracks in the jungle, so you watch for the follower and kill them on site, correct?"

"Correct sir!"

"So, you don't feel that this will be the completion of this contract then, Mr Grey?"

"Be ready for war and enjoy the peace, he would say to me over and over."

"Yes, I agree with your granddad Mr Grey, so how did he die?"

"He fell into a hold on one of the ships in the dock down the east end, broke his neck and died on the spot."

"Fell, or was he pushed?"

"Unlucky."

"Angry about that?"

Mr Grey shrugged, "It's the way he would have wanted it, he hated getting old, he could moan for England on a bad day."

Mr Black watched his eyes water and knew he had crossed the line of normal questioning.

"Sorry kid, it's none of my business."

"On the other hand, Mr Black, he would have loved you, funny name and all!"

Mr Black gave him the grin and the finger to shut up while he was ahead, then walked away in silence.

He turned back to him, "Get some rest because you're going to need it boy, we are full on tomorrow!"

"I'm sleeping in the camper van."

"Good!"

Mr Grey didn't know what else to say so he pulled out his phone and made the call.

She picked up and just the sound of her voice made him feel better, talking about his granddad made him melancholy in some way and he needed her banter to bring him round.

"Where the hell have you been, you should have phoned last night, toe rag?" she screeched at him.

"Love you babe!"

"I miss you as well, so are we done?"

"Another day and it will be sorted, but at the end of all this, we will need that bolt hole to hide in, understood?"

"But I thought that this job would sort that out the cause, yes?"

"Yes Sand, but inevitably there will be more of them asking and wanting, get it?"

He listened to her breathing for a few moments before asking the question, "Where do you think babe?"

"Well, I bloody hate Spain, to many English prats there turning oak in the sun and missing home."

"Where then?"

"America, it's a very big place Billy, we can hide there, I'm sure."

"Well, I'm still thinking Switzerland, clean air and clean people."

"Not according to these bankers, Geraldo doesn't like the Swiss, cold handshakes and hearts he calls them."

"Not nosey neighbours then Sand, that's good for us, right?"

Now she was listening to him breathing down the line, "You have another idea?"

"Na, just thinking, my only talent."

"Really?"

"Hey, I'm not phoning to be insulted."

"So, who do you normally phone to be insulted then?"

"On the plane home tomorrow night, ok?"

"Ok, babe, bring us a stick of rock."

"Sandra, this is not Brighton."

"Well, whatever then, just something, ok?"

"Ok babe, nighty night!"

CHAPTER 33 ... ASSEMBLY YARD ... ROAD WORKS ... FLORIDA.

The place was now fully illuminated as the lads sorted out their last minuet jobs, Mr Black walked into the middle of them and looked at his watch.

"To live the life, we pay ......?"

"The price!" said everyone in unison.

"No excuses, no moans and groans, we do the job and complete the contract, then we disperse, and I hope I never see you ugly bastards ever again, clear?"

"Clear!" shouted the colour men, they were ready to go.

Mr Grey watched them closely and were like grey hounds on the track ready to start barking to be let off their leash.

Mr Black looked at his watch again, "Ok, Mr Green and Mr Brown, be gone and block the road, anyone inside your picket lines are to be shot, clear?"

"Sir!" they both echoed, before walking away and getting into their vans.

He looked at the minibus and Mr Yellow, the driver, "Ok, drop us all off then go to your shooting spot Mr Yellow, over cover everyone, we must assume that they can see us, possibly infra-red cameras all over the place so be sharp, ok, lets saddle up all the gear and clear out."

He focused on Mr Orange, "Ok, Mr Orange, light the fire now please and burn everything, dust to dust all papers, card and boxes, nothing left understand?"

"Sir!"

"Then join the Brethren in your nice little fox hole for the turkey shoot, clear?"

"Clear sir!"

He focused on Mr Blue who was still on crutches, do you need them now?"

"Err ... no sir!" he threw them to the fire Mr Orange had now started.

Mr Red nodded to the unasked question and received a nod in return.

He turned to Mr Pink, "Done the washing up son?"

"Yes sir, clean as a whistle."

He turned to them all, "It had better be gentlemen, because your records are stored somewhere and if they find a print or anything of use, then, I hope they shoot you for being bloody stupid!"

"Ok, let's go!"

They climbed into the minibus and were driven off to the road works in silence, all wondering how the night and early morning would play out.

A mile out from the target he stopped the bus, "Ok, snipers out and start digging, and silently please, we are the ones who will be making the noise, inquisitive investigators looking at the machines will be downed with silenced weapons, please try not to make it like a war zone, pop, pop, will do, confuse and stay in your holes, a no risk situation so don't panic, just do your job and all will be well.

The minibus rumbled on over the temporary road surface they had created and at the first sighting of the distant hacienda Mr Black smiled, "Ok, at last, let's just get this done, I am left, and you are right, clear Mr Grey, and for heaven's sake do not get killed, your wife might kill me if I don't bring you home."

Mr Grey gave him a nervous grin as he thought about what was about to happen, his plan had to work, or they would all be killed, he looked at the faces and they were doing and obviously thinking the same.

Mr Blacks phone buzzed in his pocket, he took it out and listened to the news from the road blockers, "Ok, Mr Brown do what you to need to do, women or no women, they are a risk, no one will make a judgement if you kill them all, clear, ok, I leave it with you but do not risk us and this contract on sentiment, your own hard-nosed responsibilities, clear?"

He closed the call and looked around, "Ok, stop looking and start doing!"

Mr black climbed up to the top of the cab as the lads fuelled up the monster and watched Mr Grey doing the same.

My Yellow and Mr Orange fitted the amour to the sides of the windscreens and engine cowling in case of lucky shots hitting them, but the vision of the drivers was diminished to just a slot to see out of.

The rear gunners mounted up and ammunition was handed to them to lock and load to be ready.

"Ok, time check and radio check, click back numbers please."

He waited for the familiar clicks of recognition from each colour and counted them off one by one.

"Ok, party time, engines starting up now and ten minutes to warm up."

"Mr Grey, ready?"

He received the normal click from his radio.

"Red and blue please?"

The double clicks followed, he looked at his watch for the final time.

"Ok, all call signs, we are on the move, ready and rolling!"

CHAPTER 34 ... ROAD TURNPIKE ... COUNTY ROAD ... FLORIDA.

Mr Brown watched the old bus come down the temporary road bumping and jumping about in the humps, the suspension springs squeaking, he put his hard hat on and stood in the road with his stop sign to halt the obvious lost tourist bus.

As the bus squealed to a halt the door swished open and he stood on the lower step to talk to the driver, "Late or early matey?"

"Late Signor, for the party, yes?" he thumbed to the ladies in the back who were very curious of the new stranger.

"Ah, lucky I stopped you then driver, because that place is doomed, no planning permission obviously, so it's booms vill this morning, he's done this before apparently."

"I don't understand, I've not been informed about all this?"

"You can't go any further, the road is blocked for safety reasons, understood?"

"But I bring the girls for the party!"

He watched Mr Brown staring at the rows of ladies.

"Working girls signor."

"Ah, sorry girls for spoiling all you fun, but work is work, right?"

"I must tell them in the hacienda," he took out his phone to make the call.

But Mr Brown shot him dead with two quick shots from his semi-automatic, then turned to the girls, and gave them the death stare to silence any screams.

"Now listen very carefully please, because this could save your lives, I am part of a contract crew, and our contract is that!"

He thumbed to the distant building and smiled, letting them settle for a second or two from the sudden shock of seeing a man being killed, "Now I have this thing about cell phones, so pass them to me please, now this is my first and only warning girls, one buzz, blip, or twinkly tune and I will kill you all!"

He let the heckler machine gun fall from his armpit on its shoulder sling down to his hand and pulled back the loader to engage, "Now this could be a special time for you girls, no one has ever seen us working before, all very exciting I can tell you, but I have a clause to keep you alive, because one squeak of a warning to that place and you will all be dead, so give me your cell phones please!"

One of the women started collecting the phones one by one as some just stared in total panic at the mad man from space.

He took his hat off and scratched his head, "Sorry to be so rude, but this is work, I'm sure you understand the rules here ladies, we are going to kill them all tonight, every one of them in there is dead, understand?"

The screech from them echoed around the bus, "Bad boy's the lot of them, right?"

He stared into their faces, "So my advice is this, sit tight, do not make any sound that would upset me, or I will kill you all, I've never killed a bus load of ladies before and I might even enjoy it, so be cool, yes?"

They were now silent and speechless, "Sorry to be so rude again, not my natural state girls, it's just work, understood?"

The woman who collected the phones placed them on the front seat and smiled at him, he smiled back, "A survivor eh? Now that's how to please me, do as I demand, look, it's only for one night so please indulge me this one time, yes?"

She smiled and focused her big brown eyes on him, "Oh, dear, what eyes, oh, I can see that you are trouble madam."

He handed over a wad of cash to her, "Now I see that you are working girls, and I don't want to spoil business, so the lady here is going to spread the dosh, clear?"

They looked at him as if he had spoken a foreign language, "Cash girls, you won't lose out by indulging me darlings, so, all understood my new rules here?"

The woman counted out the cash to each of them as he watched their reactions to his generosity, "More where that came from girls, we just need your silence, clear?"

Some of them looked at the cash in their hands and nodded automatically, he looked for tears or any emotions coming his way, "Look ladies, anyone who loved one of those is a fool, they are killers of families and children, they spread misery and death all over the world, so tonight is their night of reckoning, because they are going to meet the Devil himself close up and personal."

He watched their every move and smiled his best smile to calm any nerves, "I want you to live on ladies, so do me this favour tonight, now can I ask more politely that that?"

He flicked open his phone and punched in green, "Sir, we have a problem, unbelievably we have a bus load of prostitutes on the road, I had to stop them, they were going to the big house party apparently, so what do I do with them sir?"

"Yes sir, the driver bit the dust, he wanted to make contact with the target."

He listened to the call as they watched this space alien talk his funny talk.

"Yes sir, clear, so my call, yes understood, but do I kill them all sir?"

"Ok, understood, leave it with me, tally ho, and good luck!"

He closed the call and looked at them again, "He says you can live, good eh, so be cool and live, make a secret call and die, one squeak or buzz, clear?"

He dragged the dead driver from his seat and let the body fall onto the side of the road, he then punched in the phone again, "Mr Yellow, one body at the side of the road, the bus driver, sorry sir for this, but I had no other option at the time, so pick up and dispose please!"

He closed the call again and looked at their confusion and realised that they had not heard his accent before, "Err .... Scottish, from Glasgow, Scotland!"

They stared at him in confused silence.

"Europe, the northern part, north of England, so, geography not a good school topic, eh?"

At last, he had laughs for his banter and he could breathe at last, "Sorry for this, but I still might kill you all, so sit tight and enjoy, yes?"

His thoughts were taken away as they could all feel the earth moving towards them, some squeaked in shock at the sudden light in their eyes.

"The Devil is on his way, so keep quiet and perhaps he won't notice us!"

A four-by-four truck rolled up to his side window and Mr Purple gave him the wide grin, Mr Brown tried to open the driver's side window, but it was stuck, he was about to smash it when the brown eyed woman leaned over him and slid it sideways, he caught her divine smell, "Oh boy you definitely are trouble girly, I can tell these things."

He shouted out of the window, "Yes, what?"

"The old man is on his way so be aware, if you fall you always fall into a pile of shit, a wad of cash or honey!"

"Don't be rude Mr Purple, contract rules apply, remember?"

"Ok, pull your knickers up and hold on tight, because here we go Jock!" the truck disappeared into the darkness as more lights appeared and suddenly a monster was coming for them.

"A monster signor Jock?"

"No darling, two monsters, so shush please," he checked the faces again and saw real rear as the monsters came on towards them, but then just as suddenly they turned away and all they could see was the clouds of diesel fumes billowing away in the night.

He jumped into the driver's seat and started the engine, he reversed the bus away from the contact side of the road under the cover of a hard-core pile, he turned back to the ladies and gave them the finger over the lips mime as the shooting started in the distance.

"Are we going to be friend's darling?"

"Se signor, great big friends!"

"I do love working with professionals!"

CHAPTER 35 ... THE ROUGH ROAD TO THE HACIENDA.

Mr Blacks D11 turned into the road to the hacienda complex, but Mr Greys vehicle was going faster than needed.

"Mr Grey!" he screeched into his headset, "Slow bloody down and put the bucket a foot off the ground before we hit the compound walls, clear?"

Silence from the other D11, made him suddenly panic, "Switch the damn mic on you moron!"

"Hello boss!"

"Front bucket, a foot from the floor as we hit the gates, then smash everything and anything, and bloody slow down, this is not a race, clear?"

"Clear boss!"

"Red and Blue, ready for action?"

Mr Blue clicked the mic twice in acknowledgement.

Mr Red was being sick with the movement, "I'm bastard seasick back here, just get it done!"

"Fire when fired on, of if you just feel like it!"

"Sir!"

The gate guards were confused at the lost bulldozers and pointed back to the road before being dropped by gunfire from the marshland.

Others stood to take their place but were in turn shot and killed by the sniper teams, one of the guards produced an anti-tank rocket launcher but ran out of time as he and the weapon were run over by Mr Grey and his D11, heading for the gate house.

Mr Grey's D11 took out the gate house as Mr Black's D11 headed for the secondary houses, gunfire suddenly started up from the second house, so he turned and smashed into them, driving the whole section onto the tennis court and garden, then rolling over the top of the rubble, crushing bodies and brickwork into the ground.

Mr Grey ran straight over the gate house and didn't feel any movement in the suspension of the D11 and carried on towards the main house.

Firing continued as the D11's rumbled on and the occasional ping as a bullet pinged of the steelwork sides.

Then suddenly the electric cannons in the back buckets stared firing, at any movement of men were cut to pieces as they ran.

The noise of the sniper cover was drowned out by the sound of the D11's crushing life and bricks into the soil and turf.

Mr Grey had now hit the main house and pushed the whole section of the main building into the swimming pool taking out ornate Greek sculptures and Roman columns with it, then reversing back over the rubble to finish the job.

People were running all over the place but were being dopped by gunfire, the colour men had abandoned their fox holes and now moved in close and now taking shots at anyone standing.

An old man ran towards the D11 and started firing with a handgun, but Mr Grey turned, and the Mr Blue's canon cut him down, only to be run over by the other monster machine.

Mr Black had now flattened all of the building on his side of the compound, so he looked to Mr Grey's D11 to see what to down next, Mr Grey's monster still had part of the roof section on its roof but suddenly stopped and it all slid off into the ornate garden, after which Mr Grey ran over the whole lot and flattened everything in his path, the French style pillars and fruit trees were flattened and ground into the earth.

"Cease fire!" he shouted into his head mic.

Suddenly there was silence, the shooting had stopped, and the monsters were switched off.

Peace settled on the massive scene of destruction.

Mr Grey and Mr Black stopped and looked at the mayhem they had caused and the results of their nights work.

He pressed his mic again, "All call signs, report casualties and sit reps please!"

He listened to the calls coming back to him and smiled, not one injury or death, not one, he couldn't believe their luck and smiled over to the other D11, only to see Mr Grey take off his welding glasses and grin back at him.

"So, you've been driving over this lot with the world's worst glasses on your stupid head you moron!"

Mr Grey grinned back then started up the monster again and started crushing the walls into the ground.

Mr Black watched him with interest, "Not one brick laid upon another, eh? Desolation, the complete destruction and desolation of the bad and the ugly, I hope you're listening Lord Odin, because I'm done, no more blood, no more killing, I'm retired from this madness as of now!"

"Search for runners and the wounded, coup de grace please gentlemen, only we leave this place of death, two in the head for all bodies, no prisoners, clear?"

He listened to the laughing and giggling of their success and looked at Mr Grey again as he flattened everything under his monster.

The dawn was now lightening up on the eastern skyline and the D11's did their work of bulldozing rubble and blood into the environment to be flattened and levelled.

Mr Grey started moving the hard core from the road and pouring it onto the destruction site as Mr Black moved it and ran over it to grind it down to a level surface.

Mr Purple appeared with the road roller and flattened it all out to a smooth tarmac ready surface, with a cheek grin to the two monsters and the bus load of curious women.

By the time they had all finished the sun was fully up and shining into their eyes, they stopped surveyed the road system they had just created.

He sat there and looked at the new level helicopter landing stage and smiled.

Mr Grey buzzed him on his phone, "They are some used at least, Mr Black, they bind the hard core with their blood and bones, good, eh?"

He stared at him from his D11, "And you Mr Billy Bonkers are a fucking mad man, but the only real genius I have ever met, so thank you for saving my boys with your bonkers plan!"

"A pleasure sir!"

Mr Pink was now at the side of them and shouting up, "Come on, move your arses, we have to get these back to base, I have the tarmac crew here in the morning!"

Mr Black growled at him from his cab, "It's Monday morning, you moron!"

"Ah, yes, still let's be gone from here!"

"Yes, agreed!" He stared again and couldn't believe what they had achieved in such a short time, "Well, they didn't see that one coming did they lads?" he didn't realise that his mic was live and some of them answered his question.

"Ok, level up and all colours back to the yard for further instructions!"

CHAPTER 36 ... AIR TRAFFIC NEWS HELICOPTER ... DADE COUNTY RADIO.

The shrill of country and western music blasted over the airwaves as the chopper circled the county.

Good morning people, this is Dade county radio, and this is Rudy Valance with your morning traffic reports this fine Wednesday, 07.00 for those of you awake, rise and shine for those who are not, the sun is out, and Florida fun is expected so, traffic on highway 9, looks good, the road repairs are very nearly done and dusted.

We see movement of heavy lifters being moved away and the road-sign writing crew are finishing off, the build-up of traffic at this hour is light and it looks clear on the Jacksonvill turnpike, so you can get to work America, let's make this day great, so let's go!"

He turned off his mic as the chopper pilot pointed, "What Dave, what's up guy?"

Dave nosed to the new helipad.

"And, so what?"

"Well didn't that place, well, wasn't it something else the other day Rudy?"

"Where are we?"

"The Turnpike Rudy and that's the way to that big cheese Don's hacienda, right?"

"Yeah, I know that, so what?"

Dave nosed to the helipad again then looked at him.

"Shit, it's gone, but how?"

"Moved?"

"But the place was enormous, a complex of buildings, the guy owns the county man!"

"Perhaps he sold out and moved Rudy?"

"Over the weekend?"

Rudy punched in his radio connection to the news channel, "Mike, I'm in the air with the traffic chopper, and it's gone man!"

"Oh, high Rudy, so what are you saying again?"

"The Don's hacienda complex is gone!"

Mike stared laughing at him.

"Really Mike, the whole damn place is gone, it's now a heliport or something!"

"He probably sold the place, perhaps it's his new way of moving product, who are we to ask baby?"

"Mike, over a single weekend, really?"

"Yes Rudy, I'll call the cops, stay with us because they ain't going to believe this news, not a joke though, right Rudy?"

"No Mike, the place has gone, just black tarmac and white lines, as I said, it's a helicopter landing sight, perhaps he had a plan that he didn't tell anyone?"

"I'll call the cops!"

"Yes Mike, call the cops, this is very strange man!"

The helicopter flew over the road service yard as the big bulldozers were being loaded up and driven away, "Hey, even those guys are leaving man, something we said maybe?"

The helicopter moved over to another zone, and Rudy continued his report, "Ok, people, rise and shine, the freeway is clear, and the weather is beautifully normal here in paradise! Even the gators are up and swimming!"

CHAPTER 37 ... WORKS YARD ... ROAD REPAIRS MOVERS.

Mr Black stood with Mr Grey and watched Mr Pink move the D11's and all the gear onto low loaders, he was screaming and shouting at the drivers to get going and waving a piece of paper in the air as he drove the staff to work harder, "Time penalties gentlemen please!"

"He's really taken to this Mr Grey, another monster in the making, right?"

"He's our cover sir, but can he stand the pressure if he has enquiries round his neck?"

"Oh, yes, but he'll need backup eventually."

"Not you then Mr Black?"

"No, not me, I'm done here, and in this business, retired, remember?"

"Miami airport then?"

"Yes, in two days for distribution and dispersals, right?"

"Yes sir, distribution's, on the day of dispersals."

"On time Mr Grey?"

"Of course, sir, all on time, I'll get her winding up the laptop to start the downloads."

"You understand the risks of slow distribution don't you boy?"

"No need to mention that one sir, all will be done as planned."

"Good, Miami international then?"

"Yes Mr Black, Miami international!"

"Err just a question to satisfy my interest, so where are you taking all these bits of kit?"

"Oh, Texas sir, I bought a ranch down there, plenty of room and all that."

Mr Black tutted at him, "Not good trade craft you moron."

"Innocent until proved guilty, right?"

"Not in our case son, just a whiff and you will be dead."

"Understood Mr Black, I need an army then?"

Mr Black ignored his words and walked off and climbed into the yellow cab and was driven off at speed.

"He didn't even say goodbye?" he said to the wind.

"Na, he won't, something to do with the Zulu teachings," said Mr Red, "Saying goodbye is like ending your life and he intends to carry on, Zulu's never say goodbye they simply slip away from the party and say nothing, it's nothing personal, it's just him."

"Strange Mr Red?"

"Read it in a boys own manual I think, back in his youth I think."

"Really?"

"Yep, really, really."

"So, he's a Zulu then?"

"No, a Viking, you moron, couldn't you tell?"

Mr Grey watched them all depart, he smiled at them one by one as they drove off, he saluted some of them, but he had another plan rolling and it might be a bit of a shock to some of them.

Mr Pink drove off on one of the low loaders carrying a D11, Mr Grey gave him the sign for the airport in two days, Pink nodded his understanding with a smile, but waved the convoy to get going.

CHAPTER 38 ... CAR 16 ... STATE POLICE ... TURNPIKE EXIT.

The two police officers stood and looked at the open space where the complex of buildings used to be.

"Impossible, right Jonny?"

They leaned on their police car and check the map on the satellite phone.

"Here on Friday, today gone, how the hell dose that work Jonny?"

Jonny blew out a long breath as he thought about it all, "Must have moved man!"

"Swimming pool, tennis courts, five houses in a horseshoe arrangement?"

"Worth millions, right?"

Suddenly his car radio blared out at them, "Car 98, come back!"

Jonny reached in and took the receiver off its hook, "Yes sarge, what's up?"

"What's up, what's up, are you guys on drugs? The press here are going nuts, the biggest drug dealer in the country has disappeared overnight, like space aliens have sapped him up, so what do you have over there?"

"Err .... Sarge, we have nothing!"

"I don't understand, is Mack there, put him on, you asshole!"

Jonny passed over the handle, "Yes sarge?"

"What have you got there Mack?"

"Sarge, you won't believe what we've got for you, the place has gone, swimming pool, houses, tennis courts, walls, a gate house, nothing, all gone, just black tarmac and white lines, it's now a helicopter landing pad."

"Get real asshole, how the hell can that happen over the weekend?"

"Sorry sarge, but that's it, all gone, and we can now see the swamp from here, all flat, understood?"

"What the hell is this, spooks vill?"

Jonny and Mack shrugged to each other as they listened to open air.

"So, what the hell do I tell the Captain, you guys?"

"Well, it's gone sir, all of it!"

"Impossible you idiots, ok, you've got the press coming your way, I suggest blocking the road off until a real cop arrives and oversees the situation!"

"But sarge!"

"Just do it ass wipes!"

At the back of them a helicopter arrived and landed on the new helipad.

"Oh, shit here we go!"

"Why, what's up Mack?"

"CNN you numb nuts, now what the hell do we say?"

"We say nothing boss, let them see for themselves, we don't need to say anything right?"

"Mack nodded to his reasoning, "Yeah, just see for yourselves people."

People started to climb out and look around the new site.

A man followed by a camera man and a sound man with a long boom over his head started shouting into his mic, "Well, believe it or not, I'm standing on a brand new helipad, constructed over the weekend, good eh, so what's so strange about that you say, well let me tell you what's so strange about this new road extension and this new helipad, they are where the giant hacienda buildings of one on the biggest mobsters in the country was living!"

"Yes, correct, the gangster and his people are gone, where you ask? Me too, where have they gone?"

"I see police officers over there, so let's ask the obvious question here folks!"

Mack tried to look the other way, and Jonny climbed back into his squad car out of the way, but a mic was placed under his chin.

"So, officer," he looked at the officer's name tag on his shirt pocket, "Officer Sheringham, what do we have her sir?"

"Err, we are not sure what happened, it has been suggested that the man and all his people have moved, you know, vacated to allow this new feature to be constructed, after all we need more helipads don't, we sir?"

The reporter smirked at the stupid suggestion from the police officer behind his mic.

"You have no idea do you officer?"

"No sir, this was a hacienda complex before the weekend and now it's a helipad, all slightly strange don't you think?"

The man faced the cameras again, "Well there we have it for this morning's report, the police have absolutely no idea what's happening under their very noses!"

"Now just hold it right there!"

"What then, space aliens, zapped up over night?"

Mack tried to say something, but the reporter answered his phone and ignored him.

"Yes, director, gone, all of the hacienda complex, gone, missing, the cop suggested that they had been zapped by space aliens, yes boss, the whole kit and kaboodle, gone, just fresh black and white tarmac, yes sir, really, really!"

"No one has any idea sir!"

"Oh, here we go!" said Mack as the traffic started coming down the little road and the TV station vans started redirecting their aerials for the satellite.

Mack tried to hold them back, but the questions hit him hard, repeatedly, from question shouted over to him.

"I have absolutely no ideas here folks!"

One of the press men kicked a drainage pipe sticking out from the side of the tarmac and all cameras started to focus on him and the broken pipe.

"Underneath!" squeaked the reporter, "They've been buried man!"

"What, dead?"

The man nodded then looked around for other clues for buildings being there, another kicked out a house brick from the rubble near the flat road, "Buildings were here, but now they are not!"

"What the hell happened here?" screeched the reporter from CNN, "Did you say buried?"

"Well yeah, what else could have happened here? You can't move buildings like that, where are the mains and the drains and the power supply?"

One of the reporters kicked a tin box at the side of the road, "Mains connection box, external, for garden lighting and such!"

"Shit, they've been buried alive man!"

Suddenly all hell broke loose as they all started their reports to the studios around the country down their satellite phones.

The CNN reporter was handed a phone from the pilot of the helicopter, "Better answer this one Greg, New York City, a big boss, with big questions."

"Who the hell?" he asked before putting the phone to his ear, "Sir, we're here on site, yes sir, it used to be the man's mansion, a complete hacienda complex, yes sir, gone, swimming pool, tennis courts, buildings, everything, gone, flat, just tarmac covering a flat land, but it has been suggested sir, well strange I know but that they had been buried, possibly buried alive, who knows these things sir?"

He felt the wind in his ear as the man on the line slammed the phone down.

From the other side of the pad a man held up an old branch of s tree.

"An olive tree, an 80-year-old olive tree branch, part of an ancient tree!" the man screamed out.

They now, all understood what and who they were standing on.

Another reporter touched Gregs arm and nodded away to talk to him in secret.

"Ok, do we report something like this, or do we call the FED's?"

"Look, this is big, maybe the FED's are the ones who did this, get me here?"

"Shit, this is bigger than we think, ok, I'm outa here, you can have this one buddy!"

Greg walked off and climbed back into the helicopter as they watched him as the helicopter took off.

The man was now surrounded as they asked the questions.

"Ok, hold it right there, look, Greg from CNN suggested that this might be the work of the FED's, get it? They've wanted this guy for years, so maybe they just did it and to hell with his drugs cartel, and his political connections, so from their point of view, they introduce a fear factor, get me?"

White faces stared at him then walked off, all now fully understanding the delicacy of the place and the political fallout of being there, within minutes the place was empty, and the two cops looked on bemused at the action and now the silence of the place.

"So, this place is a cemetery then Jonny?"

"What, under our feet?"

"Yep!"

"So, these guys were killed and buried?"

"Yep!"

"But who the hell could do such a thing?"

"Well one of those guys suggested that the FED's did all this, or the agency, know what I mean man?"

"Ordered from the top floor then?"

"Oh yes, the very top White House floor!"

"Ok, so are we done here?"

"Oh, yes, let's go and look at the traffic, this is the place of the dead man!"

"Agreed man!"

CHAPTER 39 ... MIAMI INTERNATIONAL AIRPORT ... FLORIDA.

Mr Grey watched the action from the viewing balcony drinking a coke, Mr Blue and Mr Red joined him and sat down at his table.

"Pay day gentlemen?"

"Yes please, Mr Grey."

He pulled out his phone and punched in the London number, "Hiya Sand!"

"Where the hell have you been toe rag, you said you'd be here two days ago?"

"Yeah, sorry Babe, they got me driving again, anyway, we need to start the transfers, the job is done, and they need paying, clear darling?"

"To your satisfaction Billy?"

"Yes sweetheart, to my satisfaction, get rolling could you darling, ping them to me and I'll sign them off one by one, yes?"

"Ok Billy, I'll on the job, give me five!"

He closed the call and smiled t them, "So, no payment and I would be dead, yes?"

Mr Blue burst out laughing.

"What, that's funny?"

"No, he is!" he nodded to Mr Green with his alligator strapped to the back of his suitcase.

"The tourist going home, suntan and sadness, craving the drinks and food on the plane."

Suddenly Billy could see them all mingling and looking up to him now and again, he smiled down at them and made the sign for a clock ticking, so to be patient.

His phone pinging made him jump, but he looked at the payment and signed it off, then watched Mr Black receive his notification call, he nodded up to them than disappeared into the toilets.

"That's one gent's!"

He watched them all, one by one taking their very important call and clarification of the new bank statements, they looked up one by one and smiled, then waked off into oblivion.

Mr Blue was giving him some information of the colours as they walked off.

"Mr Brown has a bus full of ladies and has great big plans, just stay away from the drink you crazy Jock!"

Mr Purple looked up from his little golf transport cart as it silently whizzed past.

"He's bought an airline, bonkers really, don't you think Mr Grey?"

"A pilot then?"

"Oh yes, used to be with the RAF before his troubles." said Mr Red.

"Really, what troubles?"

Blue and Red both looked him in the eyes, but he finished their sentences for them.

"Shut the fuck up!"

He didn't see Mr Black come out of the toilets, so he got up and went down there to see for himself, in the toilets it was empty of people but an overflowing trash bin, he lifted the lid and looked in, only to find, lots of grey hair and clothes.

Back on the viewing level he told the lads, but then spotted a bald, man in a red track suit sitting on a transport bus to be taken to the plane, the clean-shaven man scratched his head with his middle finger, then put his baseball cap on and turned away, the Viking moustache had gone, he looked like a different man.

"Keep safe Mr Black and I hope not to see you soon."

Mr Red was checking his bank account as he was speaking, "He has to officially resign, so he might be pulled back into the slot, nasty people you know?"

"Do I?"

Mr Red grinned to shut him up asking.

"Mr Blues phone pings his new account numbers as Billy signed it off."

He watched them closely, "So, where to now then gentlemen?"

They both looked at him expectantly.

"So, need a job lad's?"

"We thought you'd never ask Mr Grey?"

"So, what's the new plan boss?" asked Mr Red.

"Well, I've been thinking."

"Thinking what?" asked Mr Red.

Billys phone buzzed into action he smiled and answered the call, "Yes Babe, all done, and I'm on the next flight out, by the way did you find a place in Switzerland?"

"Oh good, we'll talk later."

He closed the call as they stared at him, "Ah, the idea, yes?"

"Yes boss, the new idea?" asked Mr Blue.

"Well, we were just being King makers, right?"

"What, in New York city?"

"Yes, the big seat, right?"

"And?" said Mr Blue.

"Well, where's our fee?"

"Fee?"

"Yes, for giving the new big bunce the chair, get me?"

"The new Don, of New York city?"

"Yes, I thought 2 bills, too much do you think?"

The two-colour men burst out laughing as Billy's phone buzzed out again, he answered and continued to talk to Sandra, "Ok, Babe, buy the place, great, yes, hold up a mo, I'll ask."

He held the mouthpiece, "So what language do they speak over there?"

Mr Red and Mr Blue couldn't hold their screeches for laughing at him.

"I don't matter Sand, we'll lean whatever they speak, yes?"

"German!" said Mr Blue through his laughing.

"German Babe, yes, I don't know why either," he closed the call and smiled at them again.

"Hold up," said Mr Blue, "You'll need an army to go back to New York and ask for money?"

Billy held his phone and waved it around.

"But I have an army by its bank accounts, don't I lads?"

They started laughing at him again, but a new plan was now formulating in his brain.

"So anyway, where does Mr Black live?"

They couldn't hold the laughter anymore and screeched out laughing again.

"Leave it Mr Grey, leave it right there please!" said Mr Blue.

THE END ... Until next time ... the first chapter of book 2.

BILLIONS ... BOOK TWO ... RUN BILLY RUN.

CHAPTER 1 ... MENTON BEACH ... SOUTH OF FRANCE ... ONE YEAR LATER.

The man reading his paper and drinking lager under the false palm tree was enjoying the peace and quiet of a slow morning in the sun but didn't budge when another man sat down in front of him and placed his own glass down on his table.

Eventually the man with the white hat pulled the paper away from the man and smiled, "Mr Black, glad to see you in good health sir!"

"Mr White, glad to see you are also in good health, but the answer is no, whatever the task, whatever the emergency, whatever they want, no is the answer, understood sir?"

"But sir, we have a National emergency, Billy Boncour, your Mr Grey has caused an incident."

"With whom?"

"The French sir, he's causing a war with one of our closest allies."

"How?"

"He's broken the Euro, the devaluation has caused complete chaos on both sides of the channel, his work could destroy the European Union, he has a red dot on his head sir."

Mr Black could not stop his laughter as he listened, but his phone buzzed in his pocket, he took it out and looked at who was calling, then pressed green, the laughing had now stopped.

"Yes Lidia, what's up?"

"What's up, you ask me what's up?" she screamed down the line.

"Yes darling, what's the problem?"

"500 million is the problem Bloodworth boy, you have invested half our money in God only knows what, it's only because the bank just contacted me and congratulated us for our good fortune and the investment idea, well smart arse, who's ideas are we investing in?"

"Lidia, I have ...."

"No idea, you have no idea, what the hell is this, clowns are us Bloodworth?"

He looked at Mr White across the table who nodded to him.

"Hold the line Lidia, let me talk to one who might give me a clue here." He held the mouthpiece, "Well, where the hell is the little shit?"

Mr White smiled at him, "See the problem now sir, a code red file has been stamped and approved, so are you attending to the contract?"

He glared back at Mr White, before getting back to the phone call, "Yes Lidia, I have the very person who used our funds, I will sort this at source, leave it with me please."

"Thomas, this could be their hook to get you back in the slot, so think before you act, please!"

"Will do sweetheart, and I understand the reasoning for all this, how are the girls?"

"Do not try to change the subject on me Thomas Bloodworth, what the hell is this?"

"I think I'm being pulled off the fence Lidia, so hold the line please."

"Thomas, that's our emergency escape code, do you mean it?"

"Yes Lidia, not clear how this is going to go, so clear the line until I contact you again."

" When though Thomas?"

"When I get a handle on the who, the what, and the why, bare with me on this one please darling."

"It is them then?"

"Maybe, I don't know at the moment, I'll contact you as soon as I know how it's going, in the meantime, clear the line understand Lidia?"

"Yes Thomas, we'll clear the line and wait as instructed by you and only you."

"Good girl, personal security at all times, circle the wagons with the girls and wait for me to ring, clear?"

"Is it that bad Thomas?"

"Na, just the normal panic from up top, you just do as you're told, understand?"

"Keep safe please Tommy Bloodworth!"

"Will do Lidia Bloodworth!"

Mr White watched and listened until Mr Black closed his call and faced him.

"And?"

Mr White gulped at Mr Blacks full focused stare and knew he had to come up with good news and fast, "Err.... we do have a location sir."

"And?"

Mr White nodded out to sea the on the distance the red sails of a large yacht bouncing on the offshore waves.

"That's him?"

"Twin masted Bark, called the Time Waister sir!"

"That's the name of his boat?"

"Yes sir!"

"How apt!"

Mr Black focused on him again, "And your colours are not involved on this one, correct?"

"Only for backup if required sir."

"And I'll need that then?"

"He has an army sir."

Mr Black focused on him again, "Retired colours, correct?"

"Yes sir!"

"And you don't want to take out old colleagues?"

"Correct Mr Black."

"But you would if ordered, yes?"

He watched Mr Whites jawline and knew he was correct; Mr White would follow top floor orders if pushed.

"So, this is more important than I originally realised, right?"

"It is sir, It's imperative in fact."

"Yes, agreed, leave it with me please, ok with that?"

"I have 24 hours that I could stretch to 48, but that's it sir, after that it's a contract fulfilment and the red dot time, clear?"

"Yes son, very clear."

He stood up from the table and finished his lager, then walked off down the beach, Mr White watched him strip down naked and dump his clothes on the beach, then waded into the warm blue ocean and started swimming towards the yacht on the horizon, the oak-coloured beach people looked on bemused silence at his arrival, the naked walk and his departure into the blue ocean.

"Still bonkers then old man!" he mumbled to himself "Who else would consider swimming five miles naked to a meet, only Thomas Bloodworth, Mr Black in the mood, good luck old man, and sharks beware!"

His phone buzzed and he looked at the caller, "Sir?"

"Well has he engaged?"

"Yes sir, fully engaged and going for the first contact."

"And he understands what must be done?"

"As I've said before sir, he is not the same, that American contract changed him."

"So, we'll see if he's still with us then?"

"Afraid so sir."

"And your crew, secure?"

"Always sir, you know that."

"Don't let me down Mr White, the les institutions politiques, remember?"

"Sir!"

He closed the call and looked at the horizon, Mr Black had disappeared out of view, but he wanted so much to be with him and his colour men, he kicked a dustbin in frustration, "Same as, bloody left on the beach again, bastard!"

THE END OF CHAPTER ONE
BUT THE START OF ... BILLIONS ... BOOK TWO ... RUN BILLY RUN.

BY ... PERCY STEVENSON.

The second in the new series as Billy Boncour must change the systems trying to kill him and he has such a marvellous plan to stitch them all up, but takes a fancy to a statue outside parliament, he wants Oliver Cromwell for his new house in Switzerland and is determined to get it, Frank, his old boss still thinks that he's bonkers by name and bonkers by nature.

Please contact for questions and updates at: (mjjcstevenson@hotmail.co.uk)

Second book launch coming soon ... plus news of other stories rolling.

Don't miss out!

Visit the website below and you can sign up to receive emails whenever Percy Stevenson publishes a new book. There's no charge and no obligation.

https://books2read.com/r/B-A-GXFY-HQARD

Did you love *Billion's*? Then you should read *Eddy's Allotment Diaries*[1] by Percy Stevenson!

Edward Smith has a major problem that he just can't let out, in the meantime his wife Ruby has demands that he has to fulfill, and she is a Girl Guides leader, so he comes in useful, her man to get things done, everyone wants something from him, his boss wants a million bolts manufacturing for Roll Royce, the landlord of the pub wants him to kill the escaped deer from the park, all he wants is a peaceful life and to be left alone to grow his veg.

Some would call it funny, but not Eddy as the nightmare continues.

---

1. https://books2read.com/u/mdAnOl

2. https://books2read.com/u/mdAnOl

Also by Percy Stevenson

Eddy's Diaries
Eddy's Allotment Diaries

THE GHOST PLANNER SERIES
The Ghost Planner ... Book One ...The Female is More Deadly Than
the Male ...
The Ghost Planner ... Book Two ... Promotion
The Ghost Planner Book Four... Men Of War...
The Ghost Planner ... Book Five ... The Wilson's
The Ghost Planner ... Book Six ... Brethren
The Ghost Planner ... Book Seven ... Revolution
The Ghost Planner ... Book Eight ... China
The Ghost Planner ... Book Nine ... Sin's of the Just ...
The Ghost Planner ... Book Ten ... The New Man in the Big Seat
The Ghost Planner Book Eleven ... The United Continent of the
Americas ...
The Ghost Planner ... Book Twelve ... Pure Malice

Standalone
The Ghost Planner ... Book Three ... Talbot's dream ...

Billion's

.